Horror novels b

The Squ

Billy's Expe. ....

Crazy Daisy (2022)

Hotel Miramar (2023)

Rosie (2023)

Drive (Coming 2024)

Fireman (Coming 2024)

Horror short story collection
Dead Ends (2023)

Dead Ends

By

Jonathan Dunne

Dedication

To my father, Bill, who used to tell us spooky stories when we were young. Bonus points to him for scaring my cousin so badly, he wanted to abandon the sleepover.

Though lovers be lost, love shall not; And death shall have no dominion — Dylan Thomas

Dead Ends 1

Drive

The following story is to be developed as a full-length novel of the same title — Drive — due for publication in May 2024

The black Audi Quattro was at the local scrapyard. Rumours were swirling around Old Castle's grapevine, but the three friends didn't believe it... until now. Seeing was believing. They were peering at the old banger Audi through the chain-link fence, which was the last place where they saw their dear friend Kelly Monroe alive and the first place where she was found dead.

Dusk had bruised into the night. The shocked group stood huddled together, not for warmth on this freezing December night but for the fear and loneliness that lingered in the air with their fogging breaths. The old crock black Audi Quattro in the scrapyard was just visible in the illumination thrown by the last streetlight on the stretch of road known as South Quay. This location where the trio stood tonight marked the limit where the town of Old Castle ended and began. Beyond was the blackness of the countryside, where strange things happened down country lanes. But for Grace Doyle, Hazel Brennan and Shane Maguire, tonight felt like Old Castle had ended. It was only a few weeks ago when they were here with Kelly, standing at this very spot, laughing their heads off at nothing, unaware of how sweet life was and how sour it was about to become.

In tense silence, they peered through the chain-link fence. It was a macabre notion to think that an old crock car — only it was so much more than an old crock car — was a very tangible memory of their best friend, Kelly Monroe. It was surreal and frightening to think that the black car in the shadows cast by the hulking metal…on this dark, freezing night…in that lonely junkyard…was the closest thing to their deceased friend right now. That beat-up Audi was Kelly's tomb for a few hours before they found her. It was sinister. Yes, that was the word: sinister.

Grace Doyle had tears in her eyes. 'So, the rumours are true,' she said in a meek voice, not taking her eyes off that car. Grace, Hazel, and Shane had only seen the vehicle on the TV news until tonight. But Grace had overheard her mother and father talking in the kitchen and they were going on about the rumours that the police had released the impounded 'Kill Car' as it had become known around the country.

With tears in her eyes, 17-year-old Grace whispered, 'I miss Kelly.'

'I can't believe it.' Shane kept shaking his head. 'Has anyone considered the poor Monroe family? They're going through enough turmoil as it is. And Christmas is just around the corner. Talk about kicking a family when they're down.'

Grace added, 'I saw Kelly's mom in town

yesterday. She looked like a ghost.'

There was a pause as they stared at the car that stared back at them from the gloom.

'And speaking of ghosts,' mentioned Hazel, 'what if Kelly is still in there?'

Grace and Shane answered in unison, 'Shut up, Haze.'

But Hazel was too overcome with emotion to shut up. 'Kelly must've felt so alone. None of us were there to help her.'

'Haze,' said Grace, 'don't say that. There was nothing we could do.'

'Gracie, we all saw her getting into that car,' Hazel pointed out.

On the night of the 13th of November, the kids met up in the square in Old Castle as they did every Sunday evening. The only difference on that Sunday night was that Kelly Monroe took an Uber home as her parents were at the hospital in Limerick City with Kelly's grandmother after she suffered a stroke. Only it wasn't an Uber…

Shane took umbrage at what Hazel was getting at without coming out and saying it. 'Haze, we all saw her getting into that car because we all thought — and Kelly thought — it was her Uber,' snapped Shane. 'Drop it!'

'I just—'

Shane barked, 'I said drop it!'

Grace added, 'Kelly got into the car. We all saw her get into that car…'

With an ominous air, they turned to peer at the

black Audi, its bonnet peeping into the light thrown by Old Castle's last streetlight.

'…because, at that moment, it was her Uber ride.'

'I just said that,' remarked Shane.

'Yes, I know. But Hazel needs to hear things twice to understand.' Grace was getting pissed off. Hazel's heart was in the right place, but she didn't know when to drop a subject. Hazel didn't have any filters like normal people. 'Don't turn this on anyone.' Grace hid her face in her hands and bawled. Shane hugged her. It was only now that the real grieving flowed out of her, and it had taken seeing Kelly's temporary tomb to unblock whatever had blocked up inside her.

Now Shane's eyes welled with tears.

'I'm sorry.' Hazel wrapped her arms around her besties. She would've been doing well, only she had to open that thing she called her mouth. 'I just feel that we owe her something.' Hazel damn well knew Grace had more to be sorry for than the rest of them. Grace had said nothing to them, but it transpired that Kelly had sent her a text message a few minutes after she sat in the car, telling her something was wrong. Grace's mom picked her up and was on her way home when she received the first text message:

There's something wrong.

Huh?

The driver just took a different route. I'm out on the new line road now. I keep asking him why

4

we're going a different way, but he won't answer me.

The stretch of country road didn't have an official title, but the locals called it the new line road, and it was the same stretch of road that melted into the darkness just beyond the last streetlight on South Quay. Kelly sent Grace her live location, and she watched how her best friend raced along the road map in a north-westerly direction — the opposite direction to Kelly's place.

Help!

It sent shivers down Grace's spine on reading that four-letter word. She just couldn't believe it. Was this some kind of joke they were playing on her? Unfortunately for Kelly Monroe, Grace figured they were playing a practical joke on her. It wouldn't be the first time Kelly pulled a fast one on her friend. She watched Kelly's radiant face profile bomb along the country roads. Grace had little experience with Google Maps, but even she could see that Kelly's cheerful face profile was travelling far too fast on those dark, winding country roads.

Not funny! We spoke about this B4. I don't like when you play games :(

Grace was about to show her mom her phone screen when she realised that Shane's house was on the other side of the new line road. And he would be on that stretch of road on his way home now with his dad, who collected him. They had all left the square together. Hmm, if Grace knew Kelly like she thought she knew her, then this was nothing but a well-executed practical joke. Unfortunately for Kelly Monroe, the executed part of Grace's conclusion would be the only part to come true. It wasn't a joke, practical or otherwise. What jokes are practical, anyway?

They heard the deep-chested growl before the sleek, hulking Rottweiler galloped out of the shadows and launched itself at the fence with a crash. It propped up on its muscular hind legs while its clambering front paws were in line with Grace and Hazel's faces. When Buddy pulled that heart-stopping act that first night, over two years ago, they fell back from the fence, horrified and exhilarated to see such a fierce animal nearby. But over the weeks and months, the canine got used to the four friends — now three — and it was less about the fierce guard dog piece of theatre and more about the tasty dog biscuits he expected from Shane's coat pocket.

'Doesn't Trixie ever complain?' Hazel asked.

Shane and Grace laughed through their tears. It was the way she asked, genuinely wondering if Shane's Jack Russell cared when he robbed her of food.

'You've seen Trixie. She needs to go on a major

diet. She won't mind if I steal a few of her treats.' Shane fed the beast through the fence. Buddy stuck his long, wet, curling tongue through the fence and slobbered over Shane's fingers.

'Yuck!' was Hazel's reaction.

Shane fed the rest of the biscuits to Buddy. Having gobbled the tasty morsels, the canine rubbed his rump along the chain-link, seeking poking fingers to scratch his back. Shane and Hazel obliged. Grace, however, was trying to stay in this moment of…what? Forgetting her best friend who was murdered in that same car just feet away from them, Grace desperately tried to stay in this brief moment. No, that didn't sit right with her. Her smile left her face and her eyes crept back to that black car lurking in the shadows. It was strange to think this was the last place she was, in a cold old car in a scrapyard. And for a ghastly subliminal moment in time, Kelly Monroe's pale face peered out at her from behind that grubby windscreen.

Three days later, they discovered Tommy 'The Jacker' Sheehan dead in his cell under mysterious circumstances. It was a bitter-sweet moment for Old Castle. The incident caused division among people. Some wanted justice for Kelly and wished The Jacker to suffer in prison, while others maintained The Jacker's untimely demise was perfect justice for Kelly. Either way, nobody went to his funeral except the gravediggers and they spat on his coffin before back-filling that bastard right down.

A week later, on a foggy Christmas Eve, Grace, Hazel and Shane were back at the scrapyard. The Kill Car was still visible and even more so at night, as it was now parked almost directly under the cone of light thrown by the streetlamp. Shane Maguire was feeding the Rottweiler, Buddy, through the chain links while Hazel Brennan and Grace Doyle were standing there, subdued and freezing, with their matching flashing antler hair bands and scarlet lipstick. They may have been wearing Christmassy hairbands, but it didn't feel Christmassy and no amount of garish lipstick covered the melancholy hanging over Old Castle.

'I couldn't be at home watching everyone in festive spirit, drinking, eating and laughing while Kelly is here on her own.'

Grace considered Hazel's words. She agreed on everything except the part about Kelly being here at the scrapyard. Her friend always had an eccentric streak in her and she didn't want to tell her she was mistaken. Kelly wasn't here. She reserved judgement; each to their own. 'Everybody is thinking about her. I know your family is thinking about her, but they're trying to be positive and they want to be happy for you. Everybody is hurting, Haze, but nobody wants to show it.'

'It's not Christmas at the Monroe house. Every year they deck their house out in Christmas lights. This year, they have a black wreath on their front door.'

By now, everybody in town was talking about the

incompetence of the local police station and how they turned the 'Kill Car' over to the local scrapyard without considering the Monroe family's feelings. The local police station tracked down Kelly Monroe's killer and took him into custody in a supervised cell at the back of the station, waiting to be formally charged. But the consensus was that it was just part of their job to catch the killer, and that was no mean feat seeing as local weirdo Tommy 'The Jacker' Sheehan had walked into the station on Thursday afternoon and confessed to Kelly's murder. Big Tom Daly, Old Castle police sergeant and local bluegrass celebrity wasn't the flavour of the month because he had royally fucked up when he signed the paperwork to hand over the Kill Car to the local scrapyard. He had no idea that the car would end up just down the road, resulting in legal complications and the impoundment of the car inside the scrapyard until further notice. Big Tom appeared on the local TV channel, all flustered while apologising for '...any distress this may have caused.' It didn't help that he read from a script.

The so-called Kill Car became a source of dark tourism.

'The sick n' twisted are coming from all over the country to see the car,' according to the scrapyard owner, Billy McCarthy a.k.a. Billy Mac, who got sick and tired of the curious onlookers gathering along his fence, so parked the source of curiosity further back in the scrapyard, but it was still visible and drew 'the sick n' twisted'. Down at The Hound — the same pub where Big Tom drank and played with his bluegrass band, The Dickie Tickers — Billy Mac joked with his drinking buddies he was going to charge the morbidly curious to sit into the car and cash in on the dark tourism. He couldn't comprehend the fascination with an old Audi where a 17-year-old girl had been brutally murdered, but this grease monkey knew how to make money.

'My hands are blocks of fucking ice,' Grace told Hazel as she took her hands out of her parka pockets. 'Hold my hands.'

Hazel stalled. 'You just told me your hands are "blocks of fucking ice." Why would I want to hold them? My hands are stiff enough as it is.'

Grace sniggered at that. 'Y'know, I think the cables in your head are wired differently to everybody else's.'

'Thank you.'

'I'm not sure if it's a compliment,' smiled Grace. 'Hold my hands. Forget I said anything about the cold. I just need a friend right now. I think this is the loneliest night of my life.'

Hazel was taken aback when Grace burst out crying. She awkwardly hugged her friend. They locked antlers. It would've been funny in another lifetime. Hazel held Grace but at a cold distance.

Grace stiffened. 'Why are you acting weird? I'm not a cold fish.'

'What do you mean?'

'Why are you hugging me like this?' And it was then that Grace thought she felt something beneath Kelly's coat. She froze before standing back from her.

'What have you got under your coat?' Her eyes widened. 'You're hiding something and that's why you didn't want to hold hands.'

Hazel had her right hand in her pocket, grabbing onto something through the lining of the pocket. Knowing that she had been sprung, she averted her eyes from Grace.

Grace decided at that moment to come at it with a sense of humour. The situation couldn't get any worse than it already was, and they all needed cheering up. 'What ya' got in the coat, Hazel?'

Hazel paused before zipping down her coat and pulling out a square board, 18 inches wide by 12 inches high.

For a second, Grace didn't know what she was looking it until she saw the letters of the alphabet… the numbers…Yes/No…Hello/Goodbye burn-branded into the wood.

Grace exclaimed, 'What the fuck?'

Shane turned from the Rottweiler. 'Whoa! Is that what I think it is?'

'That's a Ouija board, Haze!'

Hazel nodded. 'Yes, I know.' She stuck her left hand into her left pocket and pulled out a triangular object with a large hole in the middle of it. 'This is the planchette. She can move this and speak to us through the letters and numbers she points to.'

'No fucking way!' Shane waved his arms in protest. 'I'm not going anywhere near one of those things. They fuck with your mind! They drive you insane. There are people out at The Hillside who are there because they played with a Ouija board.'

'Shane!' Hazel interrupted. 'Don't be such a drama queen. That's absurd.'

'I agree with Hazel! Ouija boards are ridiculous. So, what are you doing with one in your coat, Haze? Hmm?'

'I didn't say I don't believe him, Grace.'

Grace muttered, 'Oh, here we go. Thought it was too good to be true…'

'All I'm saying is that he's jumping to conclusions. Those people out at the psychiatric hospital are not there because they experimented with a Ouija board. They were already unstable. Maybe the Ouija board tipped them over the edge, dabbling in things they shouldn't mess with. But they would've ended up at the lunatic asylum anyway.'

And for a second there, the three teenagers were spooking themselves. The night drew silent and took on a dreamy haze.

'Let's try it. We've nothing to lose.'

Grace and Shane glanced at each other before considering whether Hazel was asking them what they thought she was asking them. In the streetlight's illumination, they saw the excitement and relish on their friend's face, her watery eyes wide with excitement.

'No fucking way,' Shane said.

'That's just creepy, Hazel.'

Hazel's chin trembled. 'I want to wish her a happy Christmas.'

Seeing Hazel break down rubbed off on Grace.

'Me too, Haze, but this isn't the way.' Sometimes, Grace needed to sit her friend down and tell her what was right from wrong, like speaking to a daughter she might have in the future. Hazel didn't possess a filter like most people did. There was no refining and what you saw is what you got.

'Please, just once. Do it for me. If I don't do this now, I'll always regret it. My gran said Kelly's still around, Gracie. If we're going to make contact, then it should be now.'

'That's crazy talk.'

'Shane, I don't expect you to understand.' Hazel turned to Grace. 'Please? Come with me. Just you and me. It was always just the three of us.'

'Hey,' Sean protested. 'That's not true.'

'It kind of is, though, Shane.'

'Well, if you're doing it, Gracie, then I'm doing it. I'm part of this group as well.'

A strange phenomenon happened to the group. Before Kelly was taken from them, the foursome was just about the least popular group in Old Castle. But after Kelly's premature death, Grace, Hazel, and Shane became the ultimate group everyone their age wanted to be part of. Now, they believed that they were dangerous and cool. The fourth member of their troop would live forever and they were the gang who hung with ghosts. It didn't get any cooler than that. At least, that's how their 17-year-old peers saw them. Kelly had become a ghost in her own absence because everybody in town knew the three kids and it was strange to see them without Kelly. She was the ghostly memory lingering behind the hangers-on. Her ghost was the product of the locals' imagination, because all they could see was Kelly when they saw the three teenagers. Kelly Monroe was the phantom itch on the amputated limb.

'I was there from the start.'

Grace dismissed Shane. Anyway, he knew he wasn't there from the beginning. Shane was a blow-in. 'What did your granny say, Haze?'

'Are you making fun of me?'

The earnestness in Grace's face did all the talking Hazel needed. 'My gran says Kelly is hanging around.'

'What, she's just like hanging around?' said Shane in mocking tones.

'Her life was taken from her; she didn't give up her life, which is what happens and that's why ghosts are happy to cross over. She doesn't know she's dead. We need to tell her.'

For the second time tonight, the three kids realised the silent night around them. Grace eyed the road leading away from Old Castle and how it disappeared into the darkness. It was the end of Old Castle right here. Santa was getting ready for take-off up at the North Pole, a sleigh full of gifts pulled by flying reindeer guided by the houses below festooned in Christmas lights…except Monroe's house which was in darkness tonight and a funereal wreath hanging where a Merry Christmas wreath should be hanging. No, Santa Claus wouldn't be visiting the Monroes this year. But here they were, the group who hung with ghosts, standing next to a scrapyard on this icy Christmas Eve and the temperatures were already dipping below zero. Even Buddy was thinking twice about his tasty treats, preferring the warmth of his cosy kennel.

'We don't need to tell her anything,' said Shane. 'She didn't ask for help. No offence, Hazel, but your granny is mediaeval. I bet she reads tea leaves because—'

'I'll do it.'

Shane swivelled around to Gracie. 'Huh? What are you talking about? Stop encouraging her, Gracie!'

'What if her gran's right? I'm going in.' Grace just realised this was something she wanted to do. She didn't have time to say goodbye. This would be her goodbye to her best friend Kelly, but she didn't want to tell Hazel that because she would only end up hurting her feelings. She didn't need a stupid Ouija board to say goodbye. 'Shane, can you give us a leg-up?'

Shane looked about him, wondering where this sudden bout of madness had come from. 'I'm not going in there!'

'Nobody asked you to,' said Grace, calculating the height of the fence, which was twice her height.

'And what are you going to do when you get over the fence?' Shane asked with raised eyebrows. 'Then what?'

Hazel answered, 'We get into that fucking car.'

Now Grace was having second thoughts. 'What if it's locked?'

'Tell yourself it won't be.'

'Oh, did your granny tell you that too?'

Grace felt sorry for Hazel. 'Leave her alone, Shane.' She was giving second thoughts to this craziness, but the hopeless expression on Hazel's face wasn't making it easy to say no and she still held onto that one last goodbye.

She threw herself at the chain-link fence. 'Come on, let's do this before I change my mind.' She hoisted her right foot. 'Shane?' She cast a furtive glance around the stretch of street called South Quay for anyone who may have felt the need to see the scrapyard curiosity on a freezing Christmas Eve.

'The coast is clear,' said Hazel with undeniable hope in her voice.

Shane complained under his breath as he meshed his fingers around Grace's slim ankle.

'On three,' said Grace. 'One…Two…Three!' And even before she hit three, she was flying upwards, her fingers hardly touching the cold chain links. Shane had driven her to the top of the fence. Now, she just had to swing her leg over, slowly does it…then lever herself down the other side…dropping the last two feet.

Despite Shane's protests, he put everything he had into propelling Grace Doyle upwards, to where he strained a back muscle — not that he was going to mention that to the girls. A part of him wanted to show Grace how strong he was. Lately, Shane was noticing Grace differently. He never thought she was pretty in a conventional sense. But under specific light conditions, like beneath the last streetlight on South Quay, for example, her wild beauty was alluring. Shane didn't understand this change of heart; maybe it had something to do with the light of the night.

Buddy was a vicious dog, but the Rottweiler had grown used to Grace and her friends and the canine trotted up to her, head-butting her thighs for scratches and rubs. As she stroked the glossy short hair of the powerful animal, she looked over her shoulder at the parked Audi Quattro. It gave her the chills. At no point did Grace Doyle realise she was breaking the law. The thought of making some kind of contact with Kelly consumed her. She didn't believe in any Ouija board nonsense, but the chance to say goodbye was enough connection for Grace. Her skin prickled as that black car watched from the shadows. She tried to see if the Audi was unlocked, but it was impossible to see if the door locks were in the up or down position.

'My turn,' said Hazel. 'Here, take this.' She handed the Ouija board to Shane as if he was her assistant.

'And what am I going to do with this?' Shane was feeling frustrated with the entire chaotic situation.
'How am I supposed to—'

'Okay, I get it.' Without warning, Hazel flung the Ouija board over the fence towards Grace. The board sailed like a frisbee up and over the fence where Grace caught it, slapping it between her palms as if it were a giant fly.

Five seconds later, Hazel Brennan was up and over

17

the chain-link fence with the help of Shane's leg-up.

The girls whispered a thank-you and turned to tip-toe to the car.

'Hey!' Shane called. 'What about me?'

'You said you didn't want to come,' said Grace.

Hazel added, 'Go home to be with your family. It's Christmas Eve.' She spoke as if she didn't have a family and Christmas Eve didn't apply to her.

Shane appeared as if he was afraid to join them, but equally afraid to go home on his own. 'I can't go home now! Somebody has to watch out for you two.'

'You sure that's all it is?' Hazel taunted.

Grace said, 'Look, c'mon if you're coming.'

Shane took one look over his shoulder before sprinting and launching himself at the fence, grabbing on halfway up and clambering to the top.

'Jesus, Shane, do you have to be so loud? You need to be more graceful like us. We didn't make a sound.' Hazel sniggered as red-faced Shane struggled to pull himself over the top and fell to the ground.

'You didn't make a sound because you didn't have to run at the fence!' Shane struggled to keep his voice to a whisper. 'You didn't have a fool to lift you like —'

'Shut up!' Grace snapped. 'Let's do this.'

The trio, with Buddy following up the rear, made their way through the pile of crushed cars to the parked black Audi Quattro — the Kill Car — looking as ominous now as it ever did. They stared at it in silence. It held a ghastly secret. The fog grew thick and came down over the scrapyard like a smoggy, funereal curtain. The air seemed to change around them. Even Buddy the Rottweiler pricked his ears and sniffed at the air. If—

A striking screech lit up the night, frightening the bejesus out of the three teenagers. They all turned in the same direction and upwards to see the silhouette of an enormous owl perched on the streetlight. The nocturnal bird's glowing amber eyes reflected in the luminescence. It was an enormous specimen and it could have been a small cloaked child standing up there on the telephone wire, watching them through the fog.

Grace was getting cold feet now. What had seemed like a good idea outside the fence terrified her. She was about to turn and run when—

'It's open!' Shane was already opening the driver's door and sitting in, but the girls noticed how he wouldn't close the door, just in case he needed to make a run for it.

Hazel took that as her cue to sit in the passenger seat next to Shane. And just like her friend, her instinct also whispered to her to keep that door wide open.

Grace was the last one standing with the Ouija board in her hand. A biting shard of inexplicable dread spliced her insides. This was feeling very wrong on every level and she wished for nothing more than to be at home, sitting by the open fire…

I miss Kelly.

…and scoffing down all sorts of goodies. Maybe even sample a festive tipple of cinnamon-and-lemon-clove mulled wine if Mom and Dad allowed her a…

Remember that night we drank the naggin of vodka down by the Arra? We laughed our heads off until you puked into the river! I'm never going to forget that night, Kelly.

…sip of the piping hot Christmassy drink. Play Snakes and Ladders with her brother, Noel…

The longest snake, a bad omen, swallowed Kelly all the way down, down, dooowwwn from square 87 to 24…

Grace Doyle took a deep breath and sat in the back seat of her best friend Kelly Monroe's tomb-on-wheels. The first thing that struck her was the stench of cigarette butts. The second thing to rise in her nostrils was the faint trace of a chemical she couldn't put her finger on…and why should she? Grace, a 17-year-old, was unaware of what luminol was and why the forensic team used it. They collected various pieces of evidence from the fake leather vinyl seats where Kelly once sat and sent desperate pleas for help to Grace. At the time, Grace thought it was a practical joke. Since when are jokes prac—

'Should we close the doors?' Shane asked from behind the wheel. 'What if something goes wrong and we have to, like, run?' It was more like: *What if we freak out and we have to, like, run?* But Shane's conscience wouldn't allow it. He was the man here. At least, that's what he liked to tell himself.

Hazel closed the passenger door in response.

Shane and Grace paused before doing the same.

Hazel commanded them to, 'Lock the doors.'

'What the fuck, Haze?' came Shane's response.

'I agree with him,' Grace said to Hazel from the back seat. 'What's with locking the doors?'

'It'll make it a little more difficult to get out when the time comes — if it comes.'

It? Speaking about Kelly in this way gave her the creeps. It's like they were about to meet someone or something who was and wasn't Kelly.

Grace met Shane's eyes in the rearview mirror.

'Okay, it's official,' announced Shane. 'Hazel is *the* scariest thing in this scrapyard tonight.'

'If we conjure something, statistics say that one of us is going to freak and run. We need to be brave.'

'The only thing I'm running from is you, Haze. And you just made that up. You mean to tell me that there are statistics about three teenagers using a Ouija board in a car where their best friend, um…' The whole dreadful circumstance came home to roost on Shane's conscience. The 17-year-looked away as the rest of his sarcastic observation dried up to a click in his throat as the weight of the air in this blackest of black cars bore down on him.

The broadening smile dropped from Grace's lips when she saw that dark realisation bloom on Shane's face. Up until now, this bad dream was just a dream. But the nightmare Kelly must have endured came alive in the car somehow, and the outline of that night terror was razor-sharp. And speaking of sharp razors, the cutting hoot of that owl out there with amber jewels for eyes sliced deep, and it wasn't an owl anymore but a conduit for Kelly's death screams—

21

The car jolted. The three teenagers spasmed and screamed. Shane shrieked louder than the girls and he would have given a castrato a bloody good run for his money. Buddy had frightened the life out of them by launching himself at the Audi Quattro, all 60-kilo bulk of him. He looked in at them through the glass, his enormous head between his front paws pushing against the driver's window, slavering all over the grubby glass.

Shane bellowed at the canine, 'You fucker, Buddy!' while Grace and Hazel came in on backing vocals with an equally colourful chorus.

The only way to get the Rottweiler away from the car was to roll down the window. Thankfully, the car was old enough to have a window lever. Shane wound down the lever and Buddy slipped downward until he pulled himself off the car. For a second, they thought the canine was going to jump up and come in on top of them through Shane's open window, all foam and slobber. But something caught the dog's attention amongst the metal wrecks.

Grace was back thinking about Kelly and how she'd sent those terrifying texts from this very seat. She looked about the car. Everything she saw was the last thing Kelly saw. A sudden bout of anger welled inside her. 'Who gives anyone the right to take another person's life? Who did The Jacker think he was?'

'Who cares?' Shane remarked. 'He's dead and gone. That's all that matters.'

'Is it though?'

'Grace, what are you talking about?' asked Shane.

Before Grace had time to expand, Hazel reminded them they needed to get a move on. 'Grace, hand me the oracle.'

'The what?'

'The orac…forget it. Hand me the Ouija board, please.' Hazel switched on her phone flashlight and pulled the planchette out of her coat pocket and asked Grace for the board, which she balanced between the seats and Grace's lap. 'Everybody put one finger on the planchette.'

Shane and Grace switched on their phone flashlights and placed their forefingers next to Hazel's, though with reticence.

'Now, each one of us asks a question. We wait for a response. If we don't get one, we move to the next person. Okay?'

'How long should we wait?'

'I don't know, Shane.' Hazel was growing a tad miffed at Shane's inane questions. 'As long as it takes.' She asked Grace if she wanted to ask the first question, but Grace declined.

'I have a question,' said Shane.

Hazel paused before nodding her approval.

'Kelly, can you hear us? I'm Shane and I'm with Grace and Hazel.'

Silence filled the car. They held their breath and stared at the tops of their fingers resting on the planchette. They were about to ask the next question when the planchette jerked. The girls looked at each other in raw terror when Shane interrupted, 'It was me! It was me. Sorry, I-I'm nervous and my hands shake when—'

'My turn,' said Hazel, shaking her head in disgust. 'Kelly, are you okay where you are?'

Again, a resounding silence filled the car. They waited for almost a minute before turning to Grace, who spoke in a meek voice, 'Kelly, we just wanted to wish you a Merry Christmas. We miss you so much.'

Shane whispered, 'That's not a question.'

The two girls threw eye daggers at hapless Shane. God, but he was dumb when he wanted to be.

'Okay, so I'll ask if that makes you happy, Shane.' An unexpected bout of nerves crept up on Grace before she asked, 'Kelly, do you remember what happened to you?'

They stared at the planchette and their fingers through their breaths, fogging out in front of them in the three LED lights. A heavy stillness floated down over them. Maybe it was a figment of their overactive imaginations, but the swirling fog grew thicker outside the windows and with it came that insulating unnatural silence that—

'What was that?' Hazel asked, growing paler. 'Did you hear it?'

The other two nodded. They all had heard the faint high-pitch screech.

'It sounded far away,' Grace observed, pulse thumping faster now. 'Look, I think we should go.'

'It was that fucking owl again!' Shane cursed.

The streetlight was just about visible through the windscreen and off to the left of the main gates.

'The owl isn't there. It—' Hazel shut her mouth when they heard that distant shriek again, one piercing scream.

The teenagers eyed each other as they realised there was something off about that deadly squeal. Grace raised her forefinger to her pursed lips. They held their breaths and waited... And there it was again, the same pitch-perfect scream that came from all around them...all around them but from *inside* the Audi Quattro. A far-off looping wail that came around every few seconds like the revolving light of a lighthouse.

'Yep, it's the owl.' Shane was trying to convince himself and the girls, and that made it even worse. 'It has flown off somewhere.'

Hazel was shaking her head. 'That wasn't the owl. We heard it screech, and this was nothing like it.'

'Hazel?' Shane wasn't sure which way to look. 'Is that...?'

Tears were in Grace's eyes now. 'That was Kelly... That's Kelly screaming, Hazel! Let's finish this.' Her skin crept beneath her clothes.

That same stomach-churning kill-scream filled the car's interior. It was coming closer. And again...and again, that horrific death cry seeped from the very axle and chassis of the Audi Quattro with a morbid story to tell. The bloodcurdling wail came around, faster and faster, like a stuck record...somebody please wake up and lift the needle and put us all out of our misery!

Hazel screamed and blocked her ears to drown out

the piercing cry. But her efforts were in vain.

Grace and Shane cried out when they saw Hazel's reaction. She was the one who brought them here. Hazel was the one who seemed to know what she was talking about with the fucking oracle! ORACLE?! When she produced the Ouija board from under her coat—

Silence…

The hair-raising, looping screams stopped and the silence that bloomed was even louder…as were their racing pulses. The three teenagers sat there, afraid of their lives to move. Traumatised, Shane turned around to gaze wide-eyed through the windscreen. The main gates were no longer visible, swallowed up in that freezing fog. It seemed as if a thick blanket of disorientating smoke surrounded the Audi Quattro. Their only point of reference was the vague ball of white illumination coming from the streetlight. 'I'm…' But Shane Maguire didn't get the chance to tell his besties that he'd had enough fun for tonight and was going home to be a good boy for Santa…

The sound that came from the 17-year-old was like nothing Grace or Hazel had ever heard.

He gagged and screamed all at once, and grabbed a hold of the steering wheel as if they were about to careen off a ledge. Shane had just seen something in the rear-view mirror while distracted by that hanging ball of light on the street outside…on the street where South Quay seemed too far away now.

Hazel lurched and screamed when she saw Shane's spasmodic reaction. Not knowing he had seen something in the mirror, she frantically looked through the windows in a desperate attempt to see what had just startled him. But the claustrophobic cloak surrounding the Kill Car prevented her from seeing anything. The only way she would see anything now was if someone popped their head up and glared in at her, crazy-eyed and grimacing, with their nose just centimetres from the grimy glass. But that was the stuff of horror movie clichés. No, the problem here was closer to home, like inside the car.

Hazel reached for her phone and waved it about in arcs, looking for the source of Shane's terror.

In the backseat, Grace, too, was craning her neck to see what her friends had seen. And just like Hazel, she grabbed her phone, hoping to shed some light on the situation. But the effect of the swinging flashlights only added to the erratic and dizzying cacophony of fear and panic.

'What did you see?!' Grace cried out.

Shane was only a statue at the steering wheel, caught in a glitch, unblinking and staring into the rearview mirror.

His eyes, Jesus but his eyes were out on stalks and Gracie watched them in the mirror's reflection.

'Shane! What is it?!' Hazel was ready to jump out the window and clambered to find the lock on the door while she kept her eyes on Shane who had gone into shutdown.

'There's someone in the back seat...' he said in a quiet voice.

Everything went silent just then. The three young

adults froze as did their LED lights.

Barely audible, Grace whispered in the backseat. 'What?'

Forgetting how to breathe, Shane whispered, 'Someone is sitting next to you…'

Grace froze. She was so petrified her head didn't want to move. But her eyes swivelled to the right. She couldn't see anything from the corner of her vision, so summoned every fibre of her being to rotate her head to the right. She turned a little more…and more until she was looking at…nothing. 'Shane, if this is your idea of a joke, then it's a bad one.' There was nobody there. And even though she couldn't see anyone, she still held her phone in that direction. Nothing.

Hazel turned around and flashed her LED light, illuminating nothing but the cheap shiny vinyl of the back seat.

'Turn off your lights,' said Shane as he switched off his.

The last thing the girls wanted to do now was switch off their phone lights, but Shane's tone of voice told them he wasn't messing around. Their lights went out together.

Shane brought his eyes back in line with the mirror…and froze again. He reached out his left hand for Hazel.

Hazel wasn't sure what to do with his hand so took it in hers. And it felt oddly comforting…until she realised he wanted her to angle the rearview mirror towards herself. So she did…and was sorry she did.

'Who the fuck is that?!' She wasn't sure whether to scream or whisper and her words came out in one agonising squeal. A silent silhouette of a person was sitting right there next to Grace Doyle. Hazel freaked and fumbled for her phone, switched on the light and swung her phone to the right-hand side of the backseat. The moment she did, the silhouette disappeared. Hazel moved her phone back and forth and that shadow figure melted into the light whenever the LED passed over it. With a quivery voice, Hazel whispered to Grace. 'There's someone here with us.'

Grace's whole body turned electric as gooseflesh erupted down along the right side of her body closest to the fourth passenger, from her right ear right down to her toes. 'Is…Is it Kelly?' she whimpered.

Shane and Hazel glimpsed each other before shaking their heads in unison.

Hazel switched off the light and looked in the rearview mirror to see the dark profile of a man, his head and shoulders framed against the vague light of night coming through the back window. She angled the mirror in her friend's direction and Grace craned her neck to peek into the mirror. There, as clear as day, or night as was the case, the still profile of a man sitting next to her.

Their instincts kicked in at once, all three teenagers reaching for the lock buttons on the doors, pulling them up. They piled out of the car, slamming the doors behind them. They ran for the gates, helter-skelter through the fog. Buddy the Rottweiler, thinking it was playtime, bounded after them, tripping them up as they sprinted for the chain-link fence. Shane got there first and was crouched and waiting by the fence for whoever arrived first. It turned out to be Hazel who pole-vaulted into Shane's waiting hands and scrambled up and over the fence without hardly touching it. No sooner had she hit the ground on the other side when Grace skidded to a stop next to Shane. She peered over her shoulder. Something didn't feel right, leaving Kelly there with that strange thing, that fourth passenger nobody could account for —

'C'mon for fuck's sake!' cried Hazel.

Grace broke from her stream of thought as Shane grabbed her and threw her up onto the fence. She yanked herself with Shane propelling her upwards with his hands accidentally finding places they wouldn't dare talk about after.

Now it was Shane's turn. He took a few steps back and ran at the fence with a leap. With feline agility, he latched onto the chain links and then pulled himself to the top with a strength he never knew he had. Too terrified to climb down the other side and in a hurry to get away from whatever they had seen in the Audi, the 17-year-old let himself fall onto the ground on the good side of the fence, winding himself with a heaving gag. The girls helped Shane to his feet and they back-pedalled away from the fence.

The trio stood under the last streetlight on South Quay, bringing their panting breaths under control. The fog had swallowed the car.

Hazel was hyperventilating. 'Wuh-What was tha-

that-that?'

Grace put her arms around her. 'We thought you knew!' Deciding humour was the best way to snap Hazel out of her trance of horror. 'You seemed to know what you were talking about with your oracle.' Grace laughed and cried, as did Hazel once she pulled herself together. The girls hugged each other while Shane stared at the car. 'We left the doors open. What if…?'

'…it gets out?' Hazel finished.

'What?' Shane didn't know what Hazel was referring to. 'Billy Mac's going to know someone went in!' His eyes widened. 'We don't even know if he has cameras!'

'Who cares, Shane! Who fucking cares about Mac's cameras?! We left a portal open.'

Shane answered back, 'We left the car open, Hazel!' Shane had already decided what they had seen was nothing more than a figment of their collective imagination. 'You think Mac's interested in some dumb portal? Money is his portal. You heard the rumours that he was thinking about charging weirdos to sit into the Audi?'

Hazel quipped, 'Weirdos like us, you mean?'

Shane back-answered, 'That's not the same, Haze, and you bloody well know that.'

'Whatever came through is still in the car. We didn't send it back.' Hazel stared off into space. 'I don't even know how to send it back!'

Grace said, 'Who cares about fucking portals and car doors? Kelly's in there! We all heard her, right?' It was a question, not an affirmation because Grace was doubting what she'd thought she'd heard. That owl sounded very close to the screech they had heard in the car. No, that owl had sounded very close. The nocturnal bird of prey had left its perch on the street light. It could've been circling above them. The place was full of rats, which was the reason it was hanging around the scrapyard.

Hazel shook her head. 'That wasn't Kelly sitting next to you, Grace.'

'There wasn't anybody sitting next to Grace,' Shane interjected. 'Our minds only told us that because we were in that situation. We heard nothing.'

'Shane, I don't care what you say. That scream had Kelly all over it. I can still hear her.' Hazel put her hands to her ears to block the scream-on-a-loop ricocheting about inside her brain. 'I heard that same scream the night Hazel was knocked down.'

A couple of boy racers knocked Hazel down a year previous when she, Kelly, and Grace were walking back from a twilit stroll along the river Arra. It would turn out Hazel would only suffer cuts and bruises. What shocked Grace the most that night wasn't Hazel being hit by a pathetic souped-up Honda Civic but by the shriek Kelly let out of her the moment the Honda's front left wing clipped Hazel who, to be fair, was out in the middle of Maiden Street when the Honda came roaring around the corner.

'Um, did any of you grab the Ouija board?' Hazel asked.

'No,' said Shane. 'I thought you had it.'

Hazel turned to Grace with a hopeful expression, but her hopes were dashed when her friend shook her head.

'I'm outta here,' said Shane.

The three traumatised friends power-walked back to town. As they left the scrapyard behind them, Grace thought she heard the pained yelp of a dog. But she'd heard one too many distressing sounds tonight to care about a dog.

As they walked back to the town square where they were to meet their parents, the trio wondered which parts of tonight's drama had been real and not real. With every quick step of their march back to Old Castle's square, the shadow figure sitting in the back seat next to Grace and the looping scream seemed more like the result of elaborate shadows, hunting distant owls and adrenaline.

They reached Old Castle's square fifteen minutes later.

'Please don't tell anyone. If news gets out that we heard Kelly screaming in the car where she was killed, how do you think Kelly's parents are going to feel? No. This goes to our graves. Promise?' Shane held out his pinky finger.

Hazel and Grace exchanged a glance before wrapping their little fingers around Shane's. It brought a smile to their faces on this dark Christmas Eve despite the town square festooned in glittery Christmas lights.

*

Buddy the Rottweiler watched the trio fizzle away into the fog. The panting dog turned and was sloping back to his kennel when his ears pricked. A scent he wasn't familiar with rose in his moist, pulsing snout. The smell wasn't the usual burnt oil, welding fumes, mud, grease, diesel or squeaking rats skittering through the rusty dead cars. No, the canine couldn't place this unnatural aroma lingering in the fog. And then Buddy's eyes picked out a hazy silent shadow next to the car from where the Tasty Treats People had fallen. A deep rumbling growl grew in the Rottweiler's chest. Buddy bared his teeth and snarled at that still silhouette. The guard dog lowered his hulking head, coiled on his rear haunches, and then launched himself at the shadow…

But something happened to the Rottweiler in mid-air. The dog yelped and tried to turn back but gravity was in the driver's seat now, driving the large dog towards that…anomaly. Buddy left the ground very much alive but was stone dead by the time his carcass hit the hard frozen ground.

Dead End

Dead Ends 2

Hanna

The 91-year-old screamed, *'Go away! I'm just an old woman living on my own!'* in her native language from the top of the wardrobe where she was perched. Her front door was going to come crashing in any second now, with the loud, sharp crack of splintering wood. She uttered more hysterical words in a dialect not even known to herself; a dead language her forefathers once used. Ironic.

In her desperation, the old woman had scrambled up onto her clothes wardrobe in her attempt to escape the greedy mercenaries who were pounding and roaring at her front door while the city below was burning all around her. The acrid stench of melting rubber rose to the top floor of the towering grey block on the wrong side of the city. Those choking fumes had been funnelling into her pulsing nostrils for days now. The stench was worse up here than it was on the snowy streets below. That bubbling black smoke ballooned from every wheel in the city. From 18-wheeler juggernauts to kids' tricycles, the government-funded mercenaries were burning every tyre to contain the enemy. The hired cruel-to-be-kind motley crew was committing genocide in the city in their fight to contain the adversary — the invisible and invincible monster. Everyone was an enemy now, and they considered everyone collateral damage in the plight to oust the lurking terror that only manifested after the damage was done, and there lay the problem. It came, it struck, it slipped away, and was long gone by the time the symptoms appeared. Friends, family, neighbours, and strangers alike had grown used to double-glancing for signs that the unspeakable horror had been and left. Nobody was safe anymore.

She lay there, panting and feral, in the narrow space between the top of the wardrobe and the ceiling in her bleak bedroom void of furnishings. The ancient lady was only vaguely aware that she was viewing her bedroom from an angle she'd never seen before. It was odd to look down on her unmade single bed from the ceiling. Odd, yet it didn't surprise her. That was strange, considering she was unaware she had been in a wheelchair until the day before yesterday.

Despite the ruckus in the hallway outside, she refused to leave her small flat on the top 13th floor of the dreary building. She had lived there all her life, was born in this very flat, and there was no such thing as an epidural in those days. No, sir. Her mother almost died as she brought the screaming baby Hanna into this godforsaken world. Now, great-grandmother Hanna would die screaming before the enemy took her out of this godforsaken world. She wouldn't bow to the mercenaries storming every block of flats on the outskirts of the city. Slowly but surely, they had closed in; the killing wave had come rolling over all of them. She was watching the war on the TV on the kitchen counter from her wheelchair…and now here she was, roosting on top of her wardrobe and not knowing how she had got up there. Hanna didn't need her wheelchair anymore, but now she could hear them in real-time, screaming that they were going to knock the door down if Hanna refused to unlock it. She could hear ten or more bellowing men and women outside in the hallway. Why would they need so many to overcome a little old lady who wouldn't harm a hair on a baby's head? She had only months to live anyway, cursed with some disease she'd gained somewhere along the way. And she wasn't thinking clearly lately. Perhaps dementia had set in; old age will do that to a person. It had a horrible way of sneaking up on older adults, tapping them on the shoulder, then screaming 'Boo!' in their faces. And the worst of all was that they didn't even realise they were old.

Through the open bedroom window, she watched the falling silent snowflakes. Hanna wouldn't have seen the peaceful snow if it wasn't for the flashes of light from the exploding bombs and rampant gunfire. The entire building shook and rumbled as those missiles took out 'nests' as they were called in the media. Yes, those missiles were taking out those who had succumbed to the invisible monster, but in taking out one, ninety-nine more neighbours also perished. It was ethnic cleansing on a whole new level of shitstorm. The mercenaries had resorted to locking the main doors on the ground floor of those apartment blocks deemed beyond help, with too many infected to justify the healthy occupants. The chances of being infected in a building where only one infected citizen lived had come down to a mathematical equation, not just bad luck: all it took was one infected individual in a building to contaminate every other neighbour. Eventually, everyone in that building succumbed to the invisible monster. The healthy jumped to their deaths knowing that they were next while others waited for missile wipe-out. Jump or missile? Eenie Meenie, Miney Mo—

An icy draught coming through Hanna's open window brought pained screams and children crying from the streets below. Sirens wailed in the distance. But other howling screams peppered the night, and it was those guttural screams that chilled the blood, human, but not quite; the demented cries coming from those who had surrendered their bodies. The old woman wasn't sure why she had her bedroom window open. All she knew was that she was coming down with something and her blood boiled. The hot flushes were more frequent now. But it was more than just the fever; she hadn't been feeling herself lately. When had this started? She didn't know. Night and day had melted into one. Hanna was panicked and confused. She needed to see Dr Kovalenko. Maybe he could prescribe a remedy for her malady. At least something to help her sleep. God knows, but she found it impossible to sleep. The old woman was so tired she couldn't even take a nap. She had grown very restless and demented, especially at night.

The wind howling around the eaves of the building changed direction, pushing a flurry of snow through the open window, alighting on her bed.

A gravelly voice brayed through her front door. 'Open the door or we will knock it down! Either way, we're coming in. You choose.'

Now that she thought about it, her flu, or whatever malady had seized her in its grip, coincided with her abandonment. Nobody came around anymore to check up on her. Even young Borysko stopped coming. The youngster used to come twice a week to fetch fresh cod from the local fishmongers. The old woman was especially fond of fish and had a sweet spot for battered cod with a generous sprinkling of salt. But she turned her nose up at anything that came from the ocean these days. The only thing that satisfied Hanna's appetite nowadays was meat — flesh. So Hanna sent the boy to the butcher at the end of the street by the letterbox, which was collecting nothing but ashes these days. But just a few days ago, the Borysko boy turned up at her door. Whatever had greeted young Borysko inspired him to pirouette on his heels like something out of the Bolshoi Ballet and scamper. That was the last she saw of him. She never understood his strange reaction. Her neighbours had deserted her and left her to rot in her wheelchair. So wasn't it just as well that she didn't need that horrible old chair any more, just like she didn't need her horrible old neighbours. Whatever about the people living on every floor of this 13-floor building, even her own family turned their backs on her, absconding before the mercenaries came and left her at their mercy.

'Traitors! My flesh and blood abandoned me!' she cried to the four walls, floor, and ceiling.

'We only want to speak with you,' came a soft female voice through the keyhole. 'We have come to help you.' They had changed their tactic, going for a more softly-softly approach.

From her vantage point, she had a view of her front door down the hallway through her bedroom door. 'I may be old, but I'm not stupid!' she bleated. Confused, Hanna's jaundiced eyes flitted from the window to the soggy bed she hadn't slept in for some time. Her breathing was haggard, and she drooled on herself, a string of saliva dripping from the drooping corners of her suck-hole mouth onto her naked flesh covered in festering wounds…and bite marks. The hot pulse of fever was running through her veins and arteries as the freezing air billowed into the bedroom, snow melting into her blankets and pillow. The stained lace curtains flapped in the icy draught.

She leapt onto the bed and peered out into the night. Far below, she could see a group gazing up at her through the heavy, falling snow. 'Is there anyone down there to save me?! Why are you all down there? Left me to die because I am old and feeble. Shame on you!' Hanna couldn't understand why her neighbours were down there. Her eyesight was sharper than ever and she picked out several familiar faces in the crowd below and she hated every one of them, every damn last one of them. 'Fedir? Bohdan? Why have you forsaken me? I am just an old woman!'

More pounding and yelling at her door; the

friendly female voice of reason gone now.

*

'Is there anyone down there to save me?! Why are you all down there?'

On the street below, the others who had evacuated the building looked up in shock. The rest of the building was in darkness except Hanna's flat at the top of the block of flats. They gasped when the old woman appeared at the window and screamed down in cracked bellows, faint on the wind. 'Fedir? Bohdan? Why have you forsaken me? I am just an old woman!'

One woman cried, 'She doesn't know! Oh, dear Jesus! She doesn't know! Shouldn't someone tell her?'

Fedir, who lived on the sixth floor, spoke in hushed tones. 'We turned our backs on her. It breaks my heart to hear her screams. She deserves respect!'

'She deserves nothing!' protested a younger woman from the seventh floor.

Bohdan, who lived with his family on the twelfth floor, below Hanna, commented, 'If you heard what my family and I have been listening to these last few nights, you wouldn't feel any guilt. That monster deserves nothing, especially respect! The grunts and screams, may God be good to us all. Unnatural! And the stink! Oh, dear Jesus in Heaven, that putrid stink coming down through the air shafts. Putrid raw meat. Enough to knock a horse! That isn't Hanna up there. It may look like her, but don't let yourself be fooled.'

Young Borysko spoke up. 'For the last fortnight,

41

Hanna has been sending me to the butcher for nothing but meat. And this is strange because she sends me to the fishmonger for fresh cod.' The boy's comment would have been amusing under different circumstances.

Borysko's mother interrupted, 'But not normal meat. Borysko, tell them.'

The 14-year-old spoke, 'The old woman asked me to get scraps for her dogs.'

'She doesn't have any bloody dogs!' exclaimed his mother. 'She hardly has room to swing a cat!'

'Go on, boy,' Fedir said. 'Tell us more.'

Borysko told his eager audience how he had visited their elderly neighbour. 'Muh-Maybe I should've knocked, but her front door was open.' At this juncture, he glanced at his mother, who nodded encouragement. 'So, I walked in…and wished I never had.' The huddled group read the horror in the boy's eyes, and could almost see what the 14-year-old laid eyes on from the front door into Hanna's kitchen. Tears came to Borysko's eyes. 'Hanna was…' he stalled, '…sitting on the kitchen table, hunched over a bloody basin. At first, I wasn't sure what I was looking at. For the moment, I thought the old woman was making sausages…'

A ripple of nervous laughter moved through the congregation.

'…until she looked over her shoulder at me with big teeth and crazy, yellow eyes! She was feasting on the raw bones and stringy entrails I brought from the butcher's! She was ripping at the guts with her teeth…but they weren't her teeth.' The child broke down into a sobbing heap. 'I-I mean, they were teeth, but they had grown too big for her mouth!'

The 14-year-old's mother interrupted, 'But Borysko, tell them why you ran screaming.' She considered the others. 'It wasn't any old raw meat…'

In dumb stupefaction, the others looked at each other.

The 14-year-old sniffled and hyperventilated. 'Sh-Sh-She wuh-was…'

'Go on, Borysko!' Fedir encouraged him. 'Spit it out, lad!'

He screamed, 'Hanna was eating herself!'

A deathly silence fell amongst the neighbours. They looked at each other in disbelief.

'She was tearing chunks out of herself while eating the meat Borysko had brought for the dogs,' Borysko's mother flashed air commas.

14-year-old Borysko sobbed. 'She couldn't see the difference between eating herself and the putrid meat. A-At first, she was biting at her lower lip.' Borysko gestured to his lower lip as if the others were unsure where a lower lip might be located. 'Then she took a chunk out of her lip…then ravaged her lips and mouth! She chewed on her fingers…' Borysko broke down again.

Fedir tried to calm the boy. 'Shh, there now, lad!'

With wide eyes, the boy's mother said, 'She ate whatever smelt of meat! Unable to distinguish between her own body and the dog scraps! She was in a frenzy!'

'Shh! Be quiet!' Bohdan looked at them with stark eyes. 'Do you all realise what this means?!' With pity in his eyes, he turned to young Borysko.

The other neighbours gawped at Bohdan, unsure of what he was getting at.

'Spit it out, man!' Fedir demanded.

Bohdan paused; his eyes never leaving the 14-year-old. Out of earshot of the child, he said, 'Hanna never left her flat. The only way she could've contracted the invisible monster was if someone had come to visit…someone who was already carrying the monster.'

The virus, nicknamed the invisible monster, had a well-known reputation for lying dormant in a host for any period before incubating, unlike other viruses that adhere to the same life-cycle period. This was what made the monster invisible — a man-made virus created by a demented lab scientist who succumbed to his ghastly creation and unleashed it on the world because he had nothing to lose. That same mad scientist was working for the government to help find a cure for cancer. Ironic.

Shock bloomed on his mother's face, and she seemed to hold in a scream just then. 'You spit poison from your lips,' hissed the 14-year-old's mother. 'How dare you talk about my boy like that! Can't you see he's the picture of health? Hmm? Look at him, Bohdan! Think before you speak next time.'

The boy became self-aware as the pale and stunned faces in the hushed group turned to look at him with disdain, pity, and curiosity. He watched how the surrounding others took a step back…then another step…and another, back-pedalling to the other side of the street, leaving just him and his mother. Everyone knew the mercenaries were culling anyone who ever associated with the infected. Bad luck if you happened to be living in the same building and this city was nothing but drab skyscrapers — everyone was living in a building with at least one infected neighbour.

They all knew what this meant. Bogdan blessed himself over and over. Then the others made signs of the cross over their foreheads and chests. They eyed each other with suspicion, wondering who amongst them carried the invisible monster.

*

The front door burst in. The deafening crack of splintering wood filled the tiny flat before a heavy silence loomed in the hallway.

'Where is it?!' Hanna heard one of them whisper.

Another said, 'It's in here somewhere. I smell it!'

In the melee, Hanna wondered what "it" was, and the "smell" they referred to. The crouching old woman froze as she listened to the creak of the leather boots come down the hallway towards her bedroom. A wheezy growl built in her chest as the group darkened her doorway. About their waists, they carried a plethora of weapons…and dear Jesus, but was that a flame-thrower slung over one of their shoulders? But the most shocking of all were the vials and syringes strapped to their belts. They wore diver's face masks attached to bottles of oxygen slung over their shoulders.

*

The sickening stench of stale piss, shit, and something putrid — rotten meat? — filled their nostrils the moment they stepped inside the suspect's flat.

One mercenary gagged and puked into his face mask on spotting the pooling stain of acrid urine and a pile of human faeces tucked away into a corner of the hallway. It was an unnerving telltale sign. Watching the cannibals never bothered him, but seeing their waste turned his stomach every time. It wasn't the fact that he was looking at human excrement. After all, he looked at the same every day when he went to the bathroom. No, it was the way the infected went to the toilet in a chosen corner of the house, like a dog might do, and neatly piled their excrement. That notion terrified him. The infected-turned-feral forgot themselves with their first instinct being to squat in the nearest corner.

They signalled to each other in silence. In pairs, they spread out. The two individuals who surveyed the bedroom didn't see the naked old woman crouched on top of the wardrobe…until she twitched and came to life.

'There's one here!' bawled one of them, pointing to the wardrobe. The group piled into the little bedroom.

'Shh! We don't want to scare it.' Followed by, 'Jesus, I would've never seen it. They have this talent for hiding in plain sight.'

The crouching figure of the old woman turned to

stare at them from the top of the wardrobe. It was a vision that would stay with them. How that wan, sunken, wrinkled face stared and hissed like a goose. The flesh around the mouth had been chewed away, leaving a constant baring new set of teeth, which no longer fit in her mouth.

One of them whispered, 'They always go to the highest point when they're threatened.'

'Classic symptoms here, boys and girls. We've got a live one.' The speaker, who appeared to be the leader of the group, asked the others to watch the open door while he approached the ajar window. He spoke softly and confidently. 'I'm just going to close the window. It's freezing here. You will get ill.'

There's an understatement…

The hag cackled and gurgled in their faces as they approached the specimen.

Before they knew what was happening, it launched itself from the top of the wardrobe…bounced onto the bed…then scrambled through the open window. Outside, it stood on the window ledge, looked over its hunched shoulder at them…and jumped.

*

On the street below, one of the women on the street screamed, 'Look!'

Everyone looked up into the falling snow to see the little old lady, Hanna, climb out through her window. The lace curtain flapped in the wind, revealing her nakedness to the onlookers below in some kind of demented peep show. They watched on in horror as the old woman levered herself onto the window ledge, thirteen floors up into the swirling snow. She peered down at them. From down here, looking up, Hanna almost seemed to be her lovable old self — just a fragile old woman with bones of glass. Yet, she was up there, in the freezing wind, as naked as the day she was born, God love her, dancing around on that window ledge when she had been in a wheelchair the last time they saw her.

'She's going to jump!' yelled Borysko's mother, already covering her son's eyes because she didn't want her 14-year-old to have nightmares where old cannibal Hanna — Cannibahanna — played the naked leading role.

The other parents in the group took that as their cue to cover their children's eyes. Some of them tried to block their ears too in their attempt to save their offspring from future traumas and syndromes, repeating hellish nightmares of suicidal old women.

But they weren't to know that if they put their children in a giant bell jar, it wouldn't matter.

No sooner had the 'Look!' warning left the woman's lips when Hanna launched herself out into the night. As she plummeted through the air, legs and arms flailing, bleating like a goat at the slaughter, the group's collective response was one of amazement at how Hanna catapulted herself away from the window ledge, akin to something out of the daemonic Olympic acrobatic diving highlights. It was terrifying and awe-inspiring in all its hellish glory. The group scattered as the old woman came down at them at the speed of sound, screaming a cackled cry, the whites of her wide stark eyes taking them in as she plummeted towards them through the silent snowflakes. It was almost beautiful in a fiendish way; a demented opera reserved for top-ranking officials in the dictatorial state of Hell.

Their elderly neighbour landed with a resounding POP! slap bang in the middle of the circle they had created. A bloody bull's eye spray of popping cartilage, splintering bone and exploding skull. It was too late for the children, even the adults, who would take this moment to their graves, which they would all be going to in less than five minutes from now, and those shallow graves would go unmarked.

What the witnesses would take from this tragedy wasn't the perfect pop! of Hanna's body on the concrete, the ejected innards and brain matter, but the lamenting croon that came from the old woman, now nothing more than a twitching pizza on icy Poloski street.

Nadya, living on the fifth floor, opened her mouth and let out a bloodcurdling shriek that pierced the night when the old woman, no longer recognisable, pulled herself up off the ice and came towards them with backwards-facing arms, bloodied face, tongue-lolling from her twisted body-corpse. Her pale flesh, pockmarked with ghastly open and infected wounds, jiggled as she snapped her jaws millimetres from the 14-year-old's warm, pulsing throat. Her wiggling saggy breasts on display were the most upsetting of all — the last female vestige of their old neighbour called Hanna. She had been a woman once upon a time. She spoke in strange tongues, then reverted to their native language. 'Borysko, my…boy. Come, I need some scraps for the dogs…' She was broken and hell-bent on getting to the 14-year-old.

By the time the mercenaries came down the thirteen stairwells of the thirteen floors, the neighbours of the building were trying to pull what was once Hanna off the boy. But the cannibal's survival instinct was stronger. She/It was about to go to work on the boy's throat when the hired soldiers roared, 'Stand back!' But the boy's mother refused, and they had to pull her off the old age pensioner eating her son. After pulling Borysko's mother to the side, they ignited their flame-throwers and directed their streams of fire towards the old woman. She flopped about in fiery rings, screaming inhumane sounds, bleating and growling as the invisible monster inside her bubbled before falling to her knees in a fireball. The neighbours in the building, along with the mercenaries, watched old Hanna from the 13th floor burn until she resembled something left for too long over the hot coals of a barbecue.

The interventionists worked swiftly, producing vials and syringes with different coloured liquids. They took samples from the specimen, having to slice deep below the charred flesh. They needed to take their samples in that precious window of opportunity during the lightning-fast metamorphosis between the living and the living-dead.

The mercenaries turned their attention to the neighbours and asked them from which building they had come.

Brief hushed glances passed between them. Before one of the adults had a chance to lie, hysterical Borysko blurted out, 'I used to get her cod at the fishmongers!'

No sooner had the confession left the unwitting boy's lips when the mercenaries exchanged a regretful look through their diver's masks.

On cue, the neighbours scampered in all directions but were subdued and rounded up before being herded down a back alley with a dead-end.

Dead End

Dead Ends 3

The Dark Web

It was around 3:15 am on Saturday when Jessica's pleasant dream slipped into a nightmare. The dream had started with Jessica and her dad in her bedroom. She was sitting in her bed, yoga style, peering up at her father standing atop a ladder as he worked on the bedroom ceiling, scraping off old paint to prepare for a fresh coat of white paint. And while he was up there, Dad was going to stick some glow-in-the-dark stars around the six-year-old's space rocket lampshade. Jessica loved anything space-related and her favourite film was E.T. and she still cried when Michael discovered the ashen alien dying in the icy waters running through a culvert.

In the dream version, that *ksh…ksh…ksh…ksh* scratching came from the sharp edge of the paint scraper on Jessica's bedroom ceiling. The six-year-old observed paint flakes as they peeled and pirouetted through the air, and landed on her bedroom floor. Her dad worked his right arm back and forth, rasping off that stubborn old paint. He was so high up that his head was almost in the clouds. And then her dream room filled with puffy clouds and all she was able to perceive was her headless father with his head in the clouds. She giggled in her sleep.

Those cumulus clouds melted away just as quickly

as they had formed. But as they fizzled away, Jessica noticed the attic hatch to the left of where her father was stripping the flaking paint. The six-year-old didn't know why she was looking at that little door in the ceiling, yet it fascinated her. But something unseen in her dream up there had caught her attention. She just didn't know it yet. Jessica stared at that chipboard hatch as if she had never seen it in her life. But that made little sense because it was one of the first things she saw in the morning when she opened her eyes and one of the last things she saw at night before closing her eyes. And with all these glowing stars on her ceiling night sky, she would notice it even more. The attic hatch was in Jessica's bedroom. The six-year-old didn't know why because when she went to her friend Lucy's birthday party, she saw that the attic door was above the upstairs landing where they were playing with Lucy's reborn babies. And her bestie Ava's house had the hatch door in the bathroom ceiling. Jessica knew that because it was above the toilet. Sometimes, when she had to use the bathroom, she imagined something opening that hatch and looking down at her. She didn't like Ava's bathroom and always held on as long as she could until she had no choice but to use Ava's toilet. Sometimes, she was so scared of her best friend's bathroom that she wet herself. Maybe that was why she was having this bad dream—

The *ksh...ksh...ksh...ksh* was growing louder now. But something strange was filtering into her dream. That rhythmic scratching filled her head as Dad worked his strong arm back and forth, back and fo——

Jessica frowned. It was weird but when Dad dropped his right arm by his side to rest it for a moment, that scratching continued for a second longer and only stopped when it — the rasping sound — realised Jessica's dad wasn't working on the ceiling. It was like playing Red Light, Green Light in the schoolyard when she would shout, 'Red light!' and spin around to catch her friends trying to sneak up behind her.

Her dad began scratching again and the *ksh...ksh... ksh* fell into tandem with his paint scraper. And now she was glad again, watching her dad working in her bedroom. It was nice to have him here with her. When Dad came in here, it was to help Jessica with her homework or perhaps pick out clothes from her wardrobe. Yes, it was——

Her dad stepped down from the ladder and grabbed his steaming mug of coffee on Jessica's dresser. But the scratching continued on the ceiling and for longer this time. How was that happening? Her dad was supping coffee and smiling at his little princess, while that raspy scratching sounded right above his head. In the haze of slumber, she realised he couldn't hear it! But she could hear it. How can Dad not hear it? In this bedroom — Jessica's world — strangely out of kilter with the rest of the world, she raised her arm in slow motion and pointed to the upside-down door in the ceiling. Jessica realised the noise wasn't coming from the ceiling; that ominous scraping was coming from *inside* the attic hatch.

There was something up there.

She tried to tell her dad that there was something up there and it wanted to come out. But unblinking Dad kept smiling at Jessica...and smiling...and *sssmmmiiiliiinnnggg*. It was only now that she realised he had come undone and was stuck in time. She screamed at Dad to do something...anything... blink for the love of Jesus! Go and see what's up there in the attic, please, but little Jessica couldn't hear her voice as she yelled and screamed. Dad smiled and held his coffee to his face, but it never touched his lips after those first few sips. Now, Dad was hiding his face behind his Happy Father's Day coffee mug, eyeing her through the mug handle. Daddy was a glitch in the spider-webbing fabric of this nightmare. Jessica thought about the hatch in Ava's bathroom ceiling and how she thought she saw that door lift a little and searing snow-white eyes looked down at her through the slit. Whether she was a world heavyweight boxing champion or a six-year-old girl who had a penchant for reborn babies, she was at her most vulnerable when sitting on the toilet, going about her business. That was the one place she was supposed to feel safe and have her privacy. But—

ksh...ksh...ksh...ksh...ksh...

Jessica woke...or did she? Was she still dreaming? Someone had switched the light out. Her bedroom was in darkness save for the shard of light coming from the hallway and the moonlight streaming through her window at the bottom of her bed. Her bedroom had grown silent and Dad wasn't here anymore. The little girl felt the creeping bristle of fear and sunk into her blankets. She listened out for that reassuring low mumble of chatter when Mom and Dad talked downstairs, but the house was quiet... except for that scratching that had escaped from her dream.

ksh...ksh...ksh...

'M—'

She was just about to call out for Mom when the ceiling chaffing suddenly stopped. It was only now that Jessica realised she was holding her breath and could feel and hear her pumping blood pulsing in her temples and the twang of her heart in her chest. She'd never thought about her heart before, and in that moment in time, she questioned how it kept going, even when she wasn't thinking about keeping it going. And—

Click...

The attic door clinked as the latch slowly opened above her. From her bed, she observed that glinting bolt slip back. The six-year-old knew that the latch could also be opened from inside the attic, just in case someone got trapped up there.

Jessica's eyes flitted to the hatch framed against the ceiling and were just about visible in the ethereal light of the moon. The six-year-old desperately wanted those glow-in-the-dark stars now to shed some friendly light on this blooming darkness in her bedroom. And come to think of it, the patch of bare ceiling where Dad had scratched off the old paint wasn't there anymore. Her dad had never touched her

56

ceiling, yet she'd seen him on top of the folding ladder, by God, wiggling back and forth as he worked the paint from the ceiling. Jessica even noticed his jiggling belly up underneath his rugby shirt from her bed. Suddenly, she was terrified, so afraid she couldn't bring herself to call out for Mom or Dad... Wait, maybe Dad was up there in the attic?

A moment of confusion flowed between sleeping and waking...

Maybe he'd gone up there and somehow got trapped? That still didn't explain the absence of a ladder. How would he have got up there without a ladder? Did somebody take it away? Jessica looked about the room, but couldn't see any ladder.

The hatch door lifted a little more...

In this shade of darkness, the six-year-old observed that slice of black widen in the ceiling as the door opened. She heard a muffled and distressed voice coming from up there. 'Jessie? Jessie, darling? Help me. I'm stuck.'

'Muh-Mom?' Jessica called out. And this time, she could hear her own voice. 'Where are you?' Mom's voice was coming from the very walls all around her. She looked about in the darkness for her dad, but Dad was gone. Such was her desperation that Jessica even confused her standing mirror for Dad. It was dark in the bedroom and shapes took on a life of their own.

'I'm up here, Sweetie. I'm stuck,' came the whispering voice. 'Look up. Can you see me?'

Jessica squirmed down into her blankets, only her peeping eyes visible now. She didn't want to look up, but something crept into view from the darkness above her. Through the hole in the hatch came a pale arm, reaching down…down…*dooowwwn* for her. It came all the way down from the ceiling, right down to her bed.

'Take my hand, Jess. I need your help up here. I'm stuck.'

There was something strange about the way Mommy-in-the-ceiling was talking. She kept saying, "I'm stuck," but it sounded like those very words were stuck. She said them with the same intonation each time, as if those words were a recording, and had been recorded in a tin can because it sounded as if Mom was speaking from inside a tin can.

The fingers on the hand at the end of the long arm wriggled right above her, even stroking her tousled hair. Girly giggles came from the hole in the ceiling. Listening to her mom laugh lit Jessica up inside, and the bedroom wasn't so dark anymore. Those titters became her glow-in-the-dark giggles.

'C'mon, Jessie, grab my hand. Someone shut the door on me. I'm stuck.'

I'm stuck…

Nothing made any sense. Jessica cowered. 'You promise?'

'I'm stuck, Jess…' came the robotic reply. It was as if those two words I'm stuck verified everything.

Going against her instinct, the six-year-old withdrew her right arm from beneath the warm bedcovers and reached up towards the jiggling fingers. Jessica, convinced she was only in a dream or helpless against her actions because she didn't know she was in a dream, took hold of the wriggling fingers and that hot, pulsing hand snapped shut around the girl's wrist. A little too tight for comfort. And before Jessica knew what was happening, she was pulled out of her bed and upwards towards the ceiling. She looked down as she left her bed below in the shadows. But no sooner was she levitating when the hand clutching her wrist turned prickly as thick, bristling hairs grew from the palm of the blanched hand. Jessica winced as she felt those needle-like hairs prick the flesh around her wrist. And with one great spurt of speed, she was going up…up…up through the ceiling and into the attic.

The long prickling arm laid the six-year-old down by the open hatch in the ceiling. Jessica watched her mom's impossibly long pale arm retract behind a few boxes of junk. As it did, the rest of the arm snapped into joints, blackened and bristled. Not that the child was privy to this information, but that perfect arachnid leg consisted of seven segments. Starting from the fat hairy body, sprouted the coxa, trochanter, femur, patella, tibia, metatarsus and tarsus. What Jessica saw with her own two eyes retreating behind that pile of junk was a six-foot-long spider's leg in all its arachnophobic glory. She peered down through the hole to her bed below. It was odd to see her bed and bedroom from this angle. It did and didn't look like her own bedroom. The six-year-old imagined this was what a spider saw when it looked down on her at night from one of the ceiling corners. Jessica still wasn't sure how she'd ended up here in the attic. 'M-Mom?'

There was no answer this time.

From beyond the cardboard boxes came that pulsing *ksh…ksh…ksh* again. It was much louder up here inside the roof. Jessica was too small to see over the junk pile, but the looming shadows cast by the low light of the motion-sensor lighting Jessica's dad installed cast strange shadows on the black roof lining above the girl's head. She watched the Shadow Show as long, spindly limbs twice her size worked in tandem, spin…spin…spinning like a spinning wheel. Jessica knew what an old spinning wheel was because her teacher, Miss Gavin, had shown them how clothes were made long ago at school that same week. The old, wrinkled woman with the headscarf working the wheel in her schoolbook gave her the creeps, but she wasn't anything like what Jessica was and wasn't seeing on this Saturday night in the attic. And speaking of that secret room right above her bed, it was only now the six-year-old saw that the timber rafters forming the internal structure of the roof were coated in enormous stretches of gummy spiderwebs stretching from one beam to another like hammocks.

She stole up to the little mountain of cardboard boxes and peered through a slit…and forgot to breathe when she realised what made that scratching sound on her ceiling. With wide disbelieving eyes, the six-year-old watched an enormous hairy-legged spider but—

'Mommy?'

60

It wasn't Mom at all; it never had been. Yes, it was her mom...kind of. There was a huge spider back there but with Mommy's head! Her eight busy arachnid legs with prickling razor-sharp bristles were spinning something with the delicacy and finesse of a master seamstress. *Ksh...ksh...ksh* came the metrical rubbing of her hind legs. With strange fascination and repulsion, Jessica watched her mother's pale face devoid of any expression as she toiled over her work. It was strange to see Mom with no arms but eight legs, in this surreal loft in the upper reaches of her brain.

Spider-Mom turned and looked at Jessica through the slit between the boxes. Eight-legged Mommy smiled at the six-year-old, holding the child's wide-eyed gaze while her legs worked independently of her. It might not have been so bad if her mom had rows of eyes like a spider, twelve peeping black eyes planted across her forehead, but she was just her same ole' mom — the face part of her, at least. Somehow, that made it worse.

'Wuh-What are you doing?'

'I'm making you a new dress, sweetie. Do you like it? Fashioned from the finest silk.'

Jessica looked at the jumble of wrapped silk on the floor. As the mom-in-the-attic weaved, the six-year-old watched the cobweb dress grow arms as the hideous creature worked on the garment.

'Are you my mommy?' With dreamlike logic, the fact that her mom had the body of an oversized arachnid didn't seem all that disturbing to the six-year-old.

The hellish vision told Jessica, 'I am the cobweb seamstress. Esteemed member of The Dark Web. I am fashioning this cobweb dress for an important guest for tonight's feast.'

The little girl smiled. 'Who is your guest?'

'You,' whispered the thing-in-the-loft, its spindly legs working faster now, spinning silk in a blur of claw-work.

Jessica clapped her hands with excitement.

'Come and sit next to me,' beckoned Spider-Mom. 'Sit on these boxes that the man in the house left here.'

At this succinct juncture, the six-year-old did question why her dream-mom would refer to her dad as "the man in the house." This seemed to have more impact on her than the fact that her mother had eight legs and lived in the attic.

For the next 20 days (or was it 20 minutes?), young Jessica watched her altered mother spin the finest cobweb dress she had ever seen — the first dress of spider silk she had ever seen. Mother's multi-tasking legs fascinated her; how they spun, stabbed and sliced those threads of silk.

The scratching stopped.

The giant Mother-Spider raised the exquisite cobweb dress to the low light with four long stubbled legs. 'Do you like it?' The seamstress spider's voice still sounded as if she were speaking into an empty tin can. Jessica thought that Mom's voice sounded like that because she was speaking from up in the attic. But now the mom-in-the-loft was here, plump, black and hairy in the dim light, not two feet from her. Yet she still sounded the same, as if she was talking to the girl from somewhere else. 'Hmm, Jess?'

Jessica nodded, amazed by the fine filigree pattern highlighted in the bulb's light. The dress pattern was a series of intricately laced cobwebs, and the more she gazed upon the design, the more it had a strange, tranquillising effect on the six-year-old.

The dream spider watched with certain relish as the entranced little girl stared at her handiwork. Her eyes flashed, and she smacked her lips. 'Try it on, Sweetie.'

'How do you know it's going to fit me?'

'I've been watching you through the door while you sleep.'

The little girl smiled and nodded. She may have smiled, but she wasn't smiling inside. With trepidation, Jessica slipped out of her Grinch PJs.

'I'm stuck,' whispered the creature for no apparent reason.

The girl looked at her mom and for a second couldn't see her mom anymore but a nightmare spider trying its best to look like Mommy. It was as if the effects of the tranquilliser were wearing off and those first slicing shards of dulled pain were being felt. 'Why do you keep saying that you're stuck?'

The clicking spider lifted one of its front claws to Mom's lips in a secretive gesture. That surreal vision of the black, prickling hooked claw held to Mommy's lips was something the child couldn't take onboard. It was all wrong on every level of her six-year-old conscience and instinct. This thing in the attic was creeping in more ways than one now. Spider-Mom stared at Jessica and the girl didn't feel so safe anymore. She glanced over her shoulder at the hole in the upside-down floor.

'Lift your arms, darling. Try on your new dress.'

Claustrophobic with crawling dread, Jessica lifted her arms. She couldn't bear to look at Mommy anymore, so closed her eyes. Out of that darkness came soft echoey, chiming, and brittle words:

Incy Wincy Spider climbed up the waterspout,
Down came the rain and washed the spider out,
Out came the sun and dried up all the rain,
So Incy Wincy Jessica climbed up to the attic
again.

That sticky, body-hugging spiderweb dress curled down over her like a snug glove.

'It tickles,' said the child. But her timid giggle dried up when the six-year-old realised there wasn't a hole for her head to pass through. Instead, it had a fitted pouch, almost like a hood, but completely enclosed. And it measured little Jessica's head with deadly precision. The creature, not fully spider nor fully Mommy, tugged the cobweb dress tightly over her head. The six-year-old girl appeared to be a smothering pint-sized bank robber.

The spider-thing crept backwards to get a proper

look at Jessica in her new cobweb dress. Its claws clicked on the raised loft floor in approval. 'Beautiful, Jessie. Welcome to the esteemed Dark Web. You are the most important guest at tonight's feast.' And that hellish entity giggled just like before when the six-year-old heard her from her bed. 'Why, without you, we don't even have a feast!'

Jessica was finding it difficult to breathe through the face mask of spider silk. And maybe it was her imagination or just part of this spreading nightmare, but she was sure the dress was getting tighter around her chest. She was sinking deeper and deeper. The silk mask stuck to her nostrils and mouth. The six-year-old felt like something in a bag in the kitchen downstairs and her mom was using a giant vacuum sealer to suck all the air out to keep her fresh in an airtight environment. All that was missing now was keeping her in storage—

The creeping perversion took hold of the little girl in its prickling clutches, then raised her high off the floor. The freak of nature levitated the flailing six-year-old to the highest point of the attic. Between two rafters, the arachni-human placed the feast, the main dish known locally as Jessica aka Jessie or Jess, into a cobweb hammock and rolled...and rolled. The wriggling child suspended in the roof beams looked like modern art to the multi-limbed admiring monstrosity. Juvenile screams were music to its ears and it couldn't help but lick its Mom-lips.

The more she tried to get away, the more entangled Jessica became. 'I'm stuck!'

These words — I'm stuck — carried resonance for the mom in the attic of Jessica's nightmare. It paused for thought. Those words came from the mists of déjà vu. In a previous lifetime, it was a spider or a mom, or a mom or a spider; it couldn't decide.

Jessica screamed, 'I want to wake up! I'm in a bad dream! You're not real! Mom?! Dad?!' She wheezed through the layers of asphyxiating silk.

Seeing the child still had a fight left in her, the behemoth reached a silent foreleg right across the loft and eased the hatch door shut. It then spurted another thread of silk from its rear end. The convulsive workings of her hind legs spun a suffocating web to silence the child's muffled cries.

'It's all a bad dream! I'm having a nightm—' Jessica's dulled words fell silent.

*

In the bedroom across the hallway, Mr Hannigan woke. Was it just a dream, or did he hear his six-year-old daughter calling out? He held his breath and listened in the darkness. From somewhere up above him, he heard a faint thud followed by a repeated *ksh...ksh...ksh* on the ceiling.

'Rats in the attic again,' he whispered.

Mrs Hannigan roused from her sleep and responded with a confused, 'Huh? Bats?'

'Rats. I think they're back. Sounds like they're having a dance-off up there.'

'Call the exterminator in the morning. By the way, mention nothing to Jessie. How many times has she told us there's something up there?'

66

'Bad dreams, that's all. Goodnight.'
'Goodnight.'

Dead End

Dead Ends 4

The Dare

Norman Childers spotted them through the bare trees. At first, he hadn't seen them when he looked out his living room window at the park below. If it wasn't for the silvery light thrown by the full moon coupled with the park lighting, he wouldn't have seen the group huddled around one of the picnic tables by the frozen lake. It was the middle of winter and that also played a hand in revealing the nocturnal picnickers through the naked horse chestnuts. Childers questioned who they were and what they were up to. He deduced that they were teenagers smoking the devil's lettuce. He checked his wristwatch to see that it was 3:34 in the morning. Something felt off. It was a school night, and it was freezing out there. If it was a weekend or a sultry summer night when all the kids were on holiday, then Childers might've said it was pretty normal to see them out there in the park, enjoying their youth. But it was an icy December Tuesday night / Wednesday morning. He couldn't think of any earthly reason why they would be there when he had never seen them on any other night. Childers was well used to peering through his window at all hours of the night, especially when he was suffering from writer's block like he was tonight.

But the problem was that Norman Childers was looking for an earthly reason when he should've been looking for an unearthly one.

'There isn't another soul down there,' Norman said to Russ, his Jack Russell, sniffing and licking his bare feet. Later, on this very night, he would be reminded of this line.

'Maybe it's you that's a little off,' Norman said to himself. 'Perhaps you've got too much time on your hands, bud? A grown man looking out his window in the middle of the night? Maybe *you* are the one with the issue, not the people over there in the park. Russ, what say you?'

The little dog was more concerned with Norman's toes.

It wasn't as if the writer was a nosey old man whose body clock had gone haywire. He was a 48-year-old suspense author with a looming deadline for his next novel. At the rate he was going, it wouldn't make a suspense novella — maybe a short story. And the only suspense right now was that strange group sitting at the picnic table in the park across the street in the middle of this freezing night. Childers never believed in writer's block, preferring to side with the idea that writer's block was only an acute symptom of a distracted or lazy writer. But, to his dismay, he discovered that writer's block was indeed a genuine phenomenon, and he was experiencing it right now, and had been for the last seven nights in a row. His imagination was nothing but a desert, with no promise of an oasis. Childers had been staring at a blank page on his MacBook screen as if he had never written a shopping list in his life, never mind a dozen bestsellers. The truth was that he hadn't even begun to write his book. He had no idea how it was supposed to start. This is why the author was looking out his window tonight, searching for inspiration that could spark an idea, inject a little suspense into his boring life and—

'Wait!' He paused. 'This is it!' He looked about him with a great sense of awe and wonder. 'It's staring me in the face!' Whoever said the world works in mysterious ways was right! Was this the suspense he was looking for? 'Okay, maybe I'm reaching, but the seed of something is here.' Norman persuaded himself because this was as good as it was going to get. The author could start his novel with an insomniac character who just happens to be a writer…who happens to be peering out his living room window right now in the middle of a chilly night, looking for inspiration for his next book, when he spots a strange group of individuals in the park. 'God, if you're tuning in right now, thank you for your mysterious ways!' Childers rejoiced. 'But wait! What happens next?'

Norman Childers sat on the windowsill for another 20 minutes, spying on the group at the picnic table whilst he waited for divine hope to deliver the rest of his suspense thriller's plot to him. But the author was only too well aware he wouldn't find anything divine in his living room. He had to create his hope. 'You need to go down there, Norm. That's what you need to do. Write what you know, isn't that the expression, Russ?'

Russ was snoring in his tatty basket by the TV.

With growing excitement, Childers realised he had his complete novel right here tonight, but to find out what happened next, he just had to go down there. On second thoughts, maybe going down there was dangerous? Norman didn't know who these people were. But make no mistake, he needed to get a closer look at these individuals without getting closer. That seemed like an impossible task until he remembered his binoculars hanging in his wardrobe. The writer had never used them much after buying them, just hung them up and forgot about them. They were a Christmas present to himself a few years back. He liked the idea of people-watching from his living room window...until he felt he was stalking and spying on passers-by.

He left the window and went to fetch the binoculars bag hanging in his bedroom wardrobe, then took up his position at the living room window again. The author raised the eyepieces to his eyes and held his breath as he zoomed into that picnic table. Childers counted four people sitting at the picnic area, two of them with their backs to him, and two more sitting on the other side of the table. Their faces were not visible to him as they had their heads bowed, focusing on something on the table.

And that was when the wordsmith felt the first flutter inside him. Childers couldn't be sure, but it seemed as if the foursome hadn't moved an inch since he first spotted them, and that had to be almost an hour ago by now; four statues sitting there in the dancing spindly shadows thrown by the branches of the bare trees around them. Then again, there was some distance between his building and the park across the street. It wasn't possible to discern much movement, but whatever they were focusing on had all their attention. Childers considered they were viewing their phones, perhaps all four playing some online video game. Yet their body language was switched off. The author debated whether to go down there. But the looming deadline for his next thriller told him he had no choice but to go down there and get a closer look. After all, now he had a gripping introduction to his latest suspense novel. Yes, it needed tweaking, but he had the seed for an influential book.

'But that book needs to germinate and grow,' he told himself. He pulled on his puffy coat and woolly hat and was about to leave when he had second thoughts. Childers was too tired. He would wait until tomorrow night when he would be more ready for them. Besides, he was barefoot. 'Jesus Christ, what's wrong with you?' he said, looking down at his feet. He took off his coat and hat and threw them on the coat perch by the door.

But as he drew the curtains on his view of the park across the street, it dawned on him that he could very well be drawing the curtains on his next book. It would be curtains for him too! It wasn't as if he could retire any time soon. His books were hardly covering his bills, and he always needed to write 'just one more book'. Who was he kidding? Sleep was the last thing on his agenda now. If Childers went to bed now, he would only stare at the ceiling, wondering what the foursome across in the park was up to. He would've given anything just to see one of them move, never mind anything else.

For the second time that night, Norman Childers put on his coat and woolly hat and pulled on his socks and boots this time. He was about to leave the flat when he looked over his shoulder. The Jack Russell was very cosy, curled up in his basket, but the dog loved a walk in the park...and Russ would provide much-needed company. 'Russ, walkies!'

The little dog raised his head on cue, then looked about. Had he heard the magic word?

'C'mon, Russ. Yes, you heard right. Let's go for walkies.' He skipped out of his basket and wagged his stump of a tail. Childers loved how his dog was always ready for a walk, no matter what time of day or night. Once the Jack Russell heard Walkies, time no longer had meaning for the canine.

It was time to find out what happened next in this novel of his.

Suspense author, Norman Childers, descended the stairwell with his Jack Russell, Russ, on a tight leash. There was a lift in the building, but the writer suffered from claustrophobia and his dog didn't appreciate the lurching lift either. But what the writer suffered more was a mild dose of misanthropy. Having to make inane small talk with the neighbours was the worst kind of claustrophobia.

He stepped outside the Georgian townhouse. The freezing air was so bitter it made his eyes water. As he carefully picked his way down the icy steps to the street, he realised just how wintry it was tonight. He hadn't appreciated it when he was upstairs looking through his window from his warm flat. But now, feeling the bite in the air caused even more consternation for Childers — those four individuals were sitting over there in the park as if it was a mild night.

He crossed Limerick City's O'Connell Street. The author liked — no, loved — to walk through the city at night when and where it differed from the daytime. Everything that looked familiar during the day took on a different shade at night. The author had a propensity for gazing up at the lit windows of the buildings as he walked by below, wondering about the people who lived inside those windows. Each window seemed like a different world to Childers at night, and he imagined what it was like to look out at O'Connell Street from those windows. He lived on the same street, but he imagined a strange version of the city he had come to know. It was like looking at a reverse image of the city in an enormous mirror. During the nocturnal hours, the writer became a stranger in the city or maybe the city became a stranger to him.

He crossed over to the park, walked through the main gates, and continued along the pathway, casting a cautious glance over his shoulder. Childers' breath fogged out before him in steamy puffs. Russ bounced along by his feet, stopping every few steps to take a sniff. Not a sound or soul could be found in the city park. The full moon illuminated the frozen surface of the small but deep lake, making it glitter. A magical, surreal quality enveloped the entire scene. But looks can be deceiving. In the furthest corner of the lake, out of view from the public, was a fresh, jagged hole in the ice. Many urban legends surrounded the lake, some legends stemming from true stories more horrifying than the urban legends they spawned. Childers was a local expert on the lake and its sinister history. Being a suspense author, he found the lake to be fascinating in a ghoulish way. It had taken lives down through the years. No, it was more than that. It had taken lives at very strategic moments with an eerie pattern and deadly accuracy. The author would like to pen a book on the history of the ominous lake one day. But for now, he had enough with his suspense novel. He already had the first few chapters of the book and it would play out just as this surreal night was playing out. It would go something like this:

Norman's main character is a suspense novelist, desperately trying to break out of his creative dry spell. To stir the creative juices, he goes for a nighttime stroll in the city he loves. He comes across four individuals in the local park playing some kind of mysterious game by the light of the moon.

And that's as far as Childers had got. To find out what happened next, he needed to get closer…

The author tensed as he approached the picnic area. They were sitting there, just as he had seen them through his living room window. But now that he was closer, he began to question if they had been as statuesque as he had first thought. The ethereal illumination coming from the full moon, coupled with the skeletal branch shadows might have created the illusion of that eerie stillness. Childers became aware of his surroundings and how abandoned the park was tonight; how nobody would ever know if anything should happen to him now. He lived alone and didn't have regular visitors. He would disappear and nobody would ever—

'Stop,' he whispered to himself. He was about to turn back when he convinced himself to go on, finding inspiration in the knowing that the events of tonight could make or break his future.

Norman Childers wasn't to know just how true this would turn out to be.

He held his breath as he approached the picnic table, listening out for voices. But it was difficult to hear anything as the steady breeze blew through the overhead branches. Childers would've liked to hear voices, even if those voices were threatening towards him. He didn't care. But the unnerving silence coming from that picnic table was far more frightening than anything any voice could say to him. The wordsmith let on that he hadn't seen them, but walked on by, one eye on the pathway ahead and the other eye on the late-night congregation. As he passed by them, they didn't acknowledge him. They sat there in that discouraging silence. Childers saw they were young people; two girls and two boys, by the looks of things. From this distance, he guessed they were about 18 years old, and that silence unnerved him even more. He'd never known teenagers to remain so quiet. As he passed by the picnic table, the only sound he heard was his footsteps. The Jack Russell skipped right by them, unaware of their existence. The author kept walking, casting furtive glances over his shoulder, half afraid one of those statues might come gunning in his direction.

He intended to walk around the lake and head back home, but his curiosity wouldn't let him. Norman needed to know what they were up to. Throwing caution to the wind, he turned and headed back the way he came. As he approached their location, he questioned whether he should tip-toe or make his presence known. The novelist decided this time he would spy on them. It would be an interesting angle for his novel.

He doubled back. Lithely on his feet, he kept to the tree line, hiding behind the thick trunks of the horse chestnuts. Within minutes, Childers had sneaked up on the group, his safety coming second place to satisfying his curiosity. A minute later, he was right behind them. Jesus in heaven. But that silence was so creepy his skin prickled. It looked as if they were playing some type of board game, perhaps chess, which was unusual considering video games like

'Five Nights at Freddy's' were all the rage. The sound of clinking glass filtered into his hearing range.

Without warning, Russ decided he no longer wanted to play Hide and Seek with his master, and the little dog left Norman's side and skipped right up to the group.

Childers cursed the canine under his breath. He watched how the Jack Russell sniffed about the picnic table, then — oh, no — pissed onto one of the boys' feet! He drew his hand to his mouth in astonishment. This behaviour was so unlike Russ. It was the first time he'd ever seen him doing that, and it shocked him. The dog just cocked his leg as if he had stopped at one of his favourite spots to mark his territory. Childers concluded this meant one of two things: either the dog had not seen the young man or he had a strange effect on the Jack Russell. He was about to chastise the dog and apologise when he realised he was supposed to be in hiding. But now a greater reason for keeping quiet was coming to the fore, and that was the succinct fact that the teenager didn't react to the warm gush of canine urine. Even stranger, none of the four people acknowledged the dog, too concentrated on something Norman couldn't see from his vantage point.

Ever so slowly, the author came out from behind the horse chestnut tree and walked towards them. It was impossible now that they wouldn't hear or see him as he stepped through the crinkling carpet of frozen dead leaves. There wasn't a cloud in the night sky and the white full moon shone down on the four picnickers…

Only there was no picnic, but a game.

Childers stepped right up to the table. The foursome didn't acknowledge him, as frozen as the lake surface they sat by. Expressionless, black and white faces. Now, he could see that the clinking glass he'd heard earlier was a spinning bottle, glinting in the moonlight as it spun at high speed. The whirling bottle was placed in the middle of a circle of scrunched-up pieces of paper. They were playing a game the writer used to play when he was a kid with the generic title Spin the Bottle, and those little balls of paper could contain anything. Perhaps he'd stumbled upon a nocturnal kissing party game. But there was no reassuring giggle or silly laughter that might accompany such a game.

And that bottle kept spinning…

No, wait, thought Childers. *Maybe they're playing a game of Truth or Dare?*

Just when the writer noticed how the bottle kept spinning, it stopped dead, pointing straight at him. The four oddly monochromatic faces turned to look up at him from the pointing bottle. The light was poor, but Childers could tell that there was something wrong with these people. As their hollow eyes and vacant expressions took him in, he thought that maybe — *maybe* — they were ill; all four sharing the same vacant symptoms. Then he considered the possibility of drug use. He might have taken a puff or two of the devil's lettuce when he was younger, but no plant from the ground could ever have this unnerving effect.

One of the two girls shifted, reminding him of an automaton coming to life. She reached over and picked up one ball of paper and handed it to the scribe. No words passed between them. Childers gulped as she placed the paper in his hand (a piece of paper he never asked for). Their fingers touched, and that was the moment the writer realised there was something wrong tonight. His fingers were so cold that they had become numb, but Norman noticed that the girl's fingers were sticks of ice. Not only that, her skin had the texture of melting ice. The other girl and two boys looked just the same, sharing that same bluish tinge and glistening in the moonlight.

Norman considered the ball of paper in his hand and noticed how it was soggy. Not sure what to do with it, he looked at them for guidance. They waited as if Childers knew what he had to do next because he was starring in his own novel. After all, he had already written the book, even the dramatic conclusion; he just didn't know it yet. Following his gut instinct, he unfolded the ball of paper. In the low light, he could make out a childish scribble in pencil. And that was something else that got under his skin; the writing was penned by a young child or an adult who couldn't write very well…or someone forgetting how to write. He squinted to get a closer look. Not sure if he'd read the words correctly, Childers got his phone out and switched on his flashlight.

Walk Across the Lake.

With a flutter of nerves, Norman Childers looked at the four people. In the few seconds it had taken to read the message, they had deteriorated even more. A horrible realisation bubbled deep inside the author, but for the love of Christ and all that was good in the world, the author refused to take the lid off that simmering pot. These kids were playing a game of Truth or Dare, at least, their version of it. And they had just dared him to walk across the frozen lake. Yes, something was bubbling inside him alright, but it wasn't coming from the simmering pot, but the bottom of that death-trap lake. Childers had even written a letter to the city council, asking for a barrier to be set up around the lake. Something else was dawning on the author, and the more he thought about it, the more lightheaded and nauseous he felt.

'No,' he shook his head. He needed to do some quick thinking here. What would the Norman Childers of his suspense novel do? He would be cunning and turn this nightmare around.

'Yes, okay,' his voice quavered. 'I…I would like to play Truth or Dare with you. But I prefer the truth option…if that's okay?' It would be funny in another lifetime. 'What would you like to know? Ask me anything, please.'

With increasing desperation, he looked down at Russ, looking up at him with an inquisitive face and beady, glistening eyes. It was strange, but at that moment, he realised Russ was only a 6-year-old Jack Russell and not the extended part of him and best friend he'd always taken the canine to be. Correction — he was the dog's best friend, but the dog was anyone's best friend if they fed him. Russ wouldn't be getting him out of this sticky situation because he was just a dog. An acute sense of loneliness struck Childers.

With zero expression, the same sweet-faced girl, now with blueish veins spider-webbing on her face, reached down and picked up another ball of paper, then handed it to him. Feeling somewhat relieved, Childers unfolded the mushy paper and shone his light on it. His insides surged as if he'd just jumped out of a plane.

Walk Across the Lake.

The same dare was penned on this piece of paper, nothing more than a messy blot. He dropped it to the ground. Shaking his head, the writer picked up the third ball of paper from the table, unfolded it, and shone his phone flashlight to read: *Walk Across the Lake*. With frozen, jittery hands, he clumsily went from ball of paper to ball of paper, right around the circle of scrunched-up papers, fifteen in all, his heart twanging harder as he uncurled each paper ball to read the same unequivocal dare:

Walk Across the Lake.

Childers took a step away and, without turning his back to them, reversed to the public path, hoping to

God to meet a passerby who had taken a night stroll. As he back-pedalled through the bed of leaves, the four suddenly spasmed into life and came barrelling towards him. Before the scribe knew what was happening, they had surrounded him. With each step they took towards him, they visibly worsened until they were nothing but animated bloated corpses. They cornered the author and gave him no choice but to step back towards the lake…

'Russ?' he called. 'Russ?!'

The Jack Russell jumped around, yapping incessantly at Childers…at Childers, not the ghosts! The author was sure the dog couldn't see them and hadn't seen them when he lifted his leg to urinate earlier. Russ was barking because the dog thought Norman was playing with him. And for a surreal moment, Childers was watching himself and imagining how he must have seemed backing away, arms raised at nothing. Why yes, of course, Russ wanted to play! He often came down to the park during the milder weather to throw the Jack Russell a frisbee and the dog was waiting for the flying disc to appear from somewhere right now.

Childers tried to make a run for it by breaking through them, but his fingers and hands sunk into their gelatinous icy bodies. *Frog spawn,* he thought. The midnight revellers felt just like the icy jelly frog spawn he used to collect from the local pond in Sheehan's field when he was a boy and watched how those tadpoles mutated, grew limbs, and lost tails. He spasmed away and looked over his shoulder at the twinkling moonlit lake. They edged him onto the cracking ice. His boots slipped and slid on the slippery surface. The barking Jack Russell placed his two paws on the ice, and very warily, took more tentative steps onto the frozen lake. No sooner had the canine all four paws on the freezing ice when his instinct told him to turn back. The little dog watched as his master slipped, flailed, and roared at nothing in front of him as he backed right out into the centre of the lake. Childers screamed for help, but nobody came. The four dead children came bearing down on the author. He tried to escape their sticky clutches, preferring to take his chances and keep moving backwards rather than forwards into that jelly-like, eye-bulging nightmare. Their eyes swelled and popped from their sockets. The writer saw how they moved with jaw-dropping ease across the icy surface…

A splintering crack split the lake in two…

'Russ?' uttered Norman Childers before dropping through the ice. Gasping and spluttering, he scrambled to get back out, but the iced corset squeezed the breath from him as he sunk in the ice-cold waters. He witnessed the infinitely disturbing image of the four teenagers slipping into another hole like slithering eels. To Childers' horror, he realised they had made that ice-barbed hole on their way *out* of the lake, whereas he just made a hole on his way *into* the lake. Four shapes circled him once before dropping into the murky waters as if they had rocks tied to their rotting feet. Childers hopelessly tried to grasp the edge of the hole, but his fingers were numb and no longer felt a part of him. As hypothermia set in, Norman had the false sensation that his body was warming up. A strange clarity came to him.

As the freezing water flooded into Childers' lungs, he recalled why he had petitioned to have the lake fenced off. The nasty urban legend swirled around this lake. How every twenty-three years, a passerby minding their own business, would somehow end up at the bottom of this lake. And it wasn't just a legend. The last tragedy was in December 2000, on a night just like this one, when four harmless kids crossed the lake at night for some ungodly reason. Their deaths were ruled an accident when the ice cracked beneath their feet, drowning the four of them. The police looked for signs of foul play in the picnic area by the lake. They came up with nothing except a worn green glass bottle and a bunch of balled-up papers with the same scrawled words:

Walk Across the Lake.

It was a dare game gone wrong — opened and shut case. But funnily enough (and there wasn't anything funny about it), back in 1977, a similar fatality happened to a woman who had decided to walk out onto the frozen lake in the middle of the night and fall through the layer of ice. What had taken her out there? She had been on her own. Just like similar fatalities every twenty-three years since 1870, there was no plausible reason why she would take her life in her own hands and even less reason to take her life. Again, no foul play. But they found an old chipped green glass bottle and a circle of scrunched papers with a scribbled dare on a picnic table with a view of the lake:

Walk Across the Lake.

And just as quickly as that moment of clarity had come upon the author, he grew confused as he was quickly overcome by that crushing ice corset and succumbed to the elements. As he lost his grip on the ice and the world as he knew it, Norman Childers' last conscious thought was that he had found the ending of his novel.

*

It was New Year's Eve when James and Maria met up in the local park to get out of their hectic houses and share a kiss before 2047 was upon them. It was a promise they'd made to themselves. The 19-year-olds wanted to share their first kiss and make it official. That way, when they were old, they would tell their grandchildren how they had been together since way back in 2046.

Only they wouldn't get the opportunity to meet their grandchildren.

As they approached their favourite picnic table where they liked to come when the sun went down, they noticed a man sitting at their table. He said nothing, just sat there, staring at a spinning green glass bottle on the picnic table before him. They noticed a ring of scrunched-up balls of paper encircling that forever-revolving bottle. The strange individual, silent and wan, gazed up at them with dark unblinking eyes as the bottle came to a sudden stop, pointing right at them. The midnight stranger handed the girl a ball of soggy paper. She unfolded the piece of paper and squinted at the careless scrawl. In a hushed voice, she read: 'Walk across the lake.'

Dead End

Dead-Ends 5

Yucky!

It was the middle of the night when the call came in.

'Hello, you're through to Lisa at 112. What's your emergency?'

A child's moaning voice came down the line of static. 'Pleeease, help us!'

My gut instinct told me it was just a bunch of idle kids with nothing else to do with their time than to make a crank call. 'Get off the line or I'll have your call traced and you'll have the police on your doorstep. Someone else might have an actual emergency and you are obstructing the line. You are breaking the l—'

'Pleeease, help us! We're just children…'

That second cry gave me pause for thought and that was the night I learnt that your gut can be wrong sometimes. I wasn't sure if it was a boy or a girl, but I broke out in goosebumps all the same. It was the way the caller whimpered. It almost sounded like someone pretending to be just children. It was creepy. 'Yes, hello what's your emergency?' I repeated. I've got used to listening to frantic people on the other end of my phone line, but something struck me about this voice in the hundreds of panicked voices I've listened to over the last twelve months since I decided I needed to save lives to save my own.

A pause came down the line before a second child spoke. 'We're here…'

'Where is "here"?'

The second voice belonged to a girl. And I was sure now the first voice was that of a boy. Judging by their voices on the line laced with odd white noise, I placed them above five but below ten years old. It was difficult to tell them apart at that age.

You know exactly how old they are, Janey…

Yes, there was something in those voices that prickled my conscience.

The boy said, 'It smells bad down here. Yucky!'

An odd echo came through my headset. My fingers trembled on the keyboard and I stopped taking notes. With a dry mouth, I asked, 'W-What are your names?' I looked about the call centre with furtive eyes, feeling nauseous as a weakness trickled down over me.

You know their names, Janey. J—

'James,' groaned the boy.

The girl wheezed, 'Megan. I can't breathe!' And that strange echo was also on the line when she spoke. They were together wherever they were.

And you know where they are…

Yes, I knew where they were. I just didn't want to admit it to myself yet. I wasn't ready for that.

The boy, James, asked, 'Why did you say your name was Lisa? You're not Lisa.'

A cold, clammy sweat broke out on my forehead on hearing that question. 'What do you mean?' I checked herself. 'Can you please tell me your emergency?' I asked, not wanting any of my colleagues in the cubicles to my left and right to hear me not following protocol.

'Your name is Janey,' whispered the girl. 'Janey Slater. The Widow Slater.' Giggles came down the line. 'You put something in our food.'

Then, in whispering unison, they repeated 'The Widow Slater… The Widow Slater… The Widow Slater…' in quick-fire, mechanical succession.

In a terrified voice, Megan added, 'Where are you? Please save us! We can't breathe! You're the only one who can save us because you're the only one who knows where we are!'

'You know where we live,' cried the boy. 'We all live at number 2—'

I screamed on cue and cut off the call before one child blurted out my home address. They record these calls, see? The conversation I'd just had was already on record! But at least I ended the call before anything self-incriminating could be recorded. I spasmed away from my desk, pulling my headset from my head and flinging it onto the table in front of me. I stumbled from my cubicle, staring wide-eyed at the headset, knowing the horror coming from inside it. The thing is this — I know there was nobody on the line. It's all my imagination, see? But sometimes it's just so real, how they sneak up and catch me unaware. I mean, so fucking real. The scariest thing in all of this is my imagination, which I will never outrun.

The other call-takers in the 112 office appeared from their cubicles, necks craning to discover the source of the commotion. Everyone witnessed their workmate, Lisa, screaming and flapping her hands about her head as if a cloud of midges were biting at her. She was an odd person and had displayed erratic behaviour from the first day she began working at the 112 call centre just over a year ago, but she had never put on a show like the one she was putting on now. They watched her run screaming from the room, looking over her shoulders with wide eyes as she bolted through the door as if someone was chasing her. Her parting gift for her colleagues were her screams as she sprinted down the hallway, and that raw fear in her stark eyes they'd all seen when she'd glanced over her shoulder to see what was chasing her — nothing. Nothing was chasing her. At least, nothing Lisa's co-workers could see.

As Lisa ran screaming from the building, the woman working in the cubicle on Lisa's right-hand side, Sonia, picked up her headset and listened. Frowning, she turned to her colleague, Joe, and handed him the headset to have a listen. That same perplexed expression bloomed on his face.

'What is that noise?' Sonia asked.

Joe answered, 'Well, it's white noise. The real question is why it's there in the first place?'

'No, I'm not talking about white noise. I thought I heard faint voices.'

Joe scrunched up his face. 'What are you talking about?' He pulled the headset on over his ears and squeezed the sponge into his ear holes. He closed his eyes and tried to drown out the surrounding white noise.

Sonia witnessed the moment on her colleague's face when he heard the same as she did.

There, very faint and lost in the warbling white noise, Joe made out voices…two voices… 'Kids?'

*

'Wakey, wakey! Rise 'n shine!'

I thought I heard a knock before the woman's voice crept through my slumbering sleep. In my confusion, I opened my eyes to see a woman sitting by my side on the bed, staring into my face. My vision was blurry, but I was aware of another individual, a man, standing at the side of the bed behind her.

'We heard you want to confess?' came a woman's voice.

'W-Who are you?' I was lost in the dregs of a comatose sleep and the Midazolam which The Hillside staff injected into my median cubital vein kept me groggy. Yes, I know what you're thinking. I could have just said vein, right? Wrong. When I was doing my research with ___ on ___ the children, I learned all about the body and how it functions. The body is a little fucking miracle, did you know that? Anyway, I got to know all the medical terms, Latin terms, for different parts of the body and how they work. It sort of stuck with me, see? It always struck me as odd how most people don't know how their own body works…but they know how to make it stop

92

working.

I asked them who they were for the second time.

The woman answered, 'We are upholders of justice.'

'Finally! Please, lock me up and throw away the key!' I cried. 'I want you to protect me from them! I'm tired of paying for my sins. They always know where to find me! They always know where to find me because they're inside my fucking head!'

'Whoa, hold your horses, Janey,' said the woman. 'What we need right now is for you to tell us everything from the very beginning, and only then can you suffer for your heinous crime.'

'Your terrible sin,' the man added.

The woman next to me touched my hair and played with my split ends.

'You haven't seen split ends before?' I asked with a cackle.

She just looked at me with that nonplussed face of hers. It was a visage I wanted to slap. 'Whatever about split ends,' I said, 'I'm at my wit's end, see, and I've gained the bad habit of plucking at my hair.' My eyesight pulled into focus and I really looked at them for the first time. 'Wait, who called you?' Something didn't feel right. I was under the influence of a tranquilliser, but I was sure I hadn't called for anyone. Or had I? Maybe the horrid matron called for them? They call her The Auld Seagull. She thinks I'm putting on a crazy act just to stay in the comfort of my padded cell, hidden from the world and the netherworld. Everything is a figment of my imagination. The scariest thing in this asylum is the matron. But this is no act, see. Those kids haunt me… but they're ghosts living in my head. They have medication for stuff like that in this place. This is the best place for me. I'm convinced it is the only place where I can protect myself from myself.

'We were called,' said the woman, not giving away any more information.

'Because you want to confess,' added the standing man. This time, it wasn't a question.

'W-Who did you say you are?'

The woman sitting on my bed said, 'You can call me One.' Gesturing behind her, 'And this is Two.'

'Don't you have names?' Why do they look familiar?'

'One and Two, that's all you need to know for now,' said the sitting woman.

Two said, ' And we're asking the questions here.'

My eyesight sharpened a little more. I wouldn't like to get on the wrong side of the one they called Two. He had a mean face and haunting eyes. I've seen those eyes before — those eyes have seen things they were never meant to see. I see those peepers every time I look in the mirror, which is why I smashed every mirror in the house. They say a broken mirror will bring the person who broke it seven years of bad luck. I've smashed four mirrors in my place over these last few days. Mathematics was never my strong point, but I made that twenty-eight years. At my age, that's a death sentence.

'So, Janey Slater,' said One, 'why don't you tell us

everything from the start? Nice n' easy does it.'

I deduced these two were detectives — smart-ass detectives, worse again. They talked like detectives, trying to be smart, but quite hollow in the brains department. Yet I was never happier to see two smart-ass detectives in all my life. The curtain was coming down on this horror show I brought upon myself.

I was about to tell them my story when I paused. 'How did you get in here?' Such a trivial detail wouldn't have bothered me, but there was a rigmarole to entering and leaving my padded cell, and I think I would've heard the jingling commotion of the locks and keys in that thick door over there with the little window.

'Don't worry your pretty little head about that,' sneered Two. 'We have certain privileges around here.'

One added, 'We can open doors where there are no doors.'

I wasn't sure I liked the sound of that.

'We're here to listen to your confession,' repeated Two.

I nodded. 'Yes, and it's better if I go to the end and work backwards. But I'm not sure which end the end is at.' I giggled like a little girl on laughing gas. Whatever mix of meds they'd given me to calm me down made my lips feel like they belonged to someone else. My mouth tingled. Yes, I must have put on one hell of a show. Between you, me, and these four padded walls, I'm not insane, see. Yes, I have my moments, like everybody else, but I'm not batshit crazy like my neighbours along this hallway. You should see what lightning and thunderstorms do to them. That's all I'll say on that matter. I just need to seem insane. That way, I keep the ghosts at bay. They follow me everywhere…except here. They cannot get through these padded walls and my firewall of tranquillisers. I am more than happy to live out my days here at The Hillside. So, I'm not mad. Get it? Wink, wink. That show you witnessed a few days ago at the 112 emergency service call centre? Remember that? It didn't happen. I just convinced myself it happened. If I can convince myself that those children's voices spoke to me through my headset, then I can convince the world that I'm not fit for society. What I'm trying to say is that I know it's all in my head, so looking at it that way, I'm in the right place here at the mental asylum, see.

Two said, 'You can start at whatever end you want as long as we get to the end. Does that make sense? It's time to own up to your deadly deeds, Slater.' He licked his lips as if those deeds were salty snacks.

'For such a noble name,' One observed, 'The Hillside isn't very noble,' referring to the psychiatric hospital overlooking the Atlantic Ocean. 'The walls of the hospital are streaked with seagull shit…'

'And graffiti where there shouldn't be any,' interjected Two. 'Have you seen the filth written inside your toilet bowl? What kind of lunatic sketches profanities down inside the U-bend of a toilet? Who would spend their time down in the sewer pipes?'

Two flashed me a strange glance just then. My

heart twanged in my chest. He knows something. They know something. She's trying to be all nice, while he dares to be a little threatening. They're playing good cop, bad cop. But they're not talented players because old Widow Slater is sharper than these two blunt objects, see.

One quipped, 'Potty mouth.'

'Okay,' I said, 'I know where you're going with this. You seem to know it all.' And even though I knew they knew what I had done, something didn't sit right with me. 'When were you looking down the toilet bowl? Why were you looking down the toilet bowl?' And that got me thinking, how long had they been in this room, watching me while I was sleeping? I came over all vulnerable. My insides fluttered. I've learnt to trust my instinct, and what my instinct was telling me now was that there was something very wrong in this padded room. My eyes crept to the camera on the ceiling in the far corner of the room. I gestured to whoever was on the other side of that lens to: 'Get down here now! Lemme out! Who are these people? Someone should be in here observing this!' And it was true. How could the hospital staff allow a couple of detectives in here without some kind of observation? I bet you the matron is behind this. The Auld Seagull is a real vindictive bitch with a wicked eye, see, and she condescends to the patients. She fuels their insanity.

'We need you to calm down now. You want this to be over, right?' One asked.

I nodded.

'Then you need to tell us your confession,' she said.

Two commented, 'Did you know rats are crawling through the shit pipes of this loony bin? Hmm? Imagine one of those things coming up out of the bowl and you feel the bristle of whiskers on your bare ass before those gnawing incisors sink into your—'

'Two,' said One, 'we're here to listen to her confession. By the way, they prefer the term psychiatric facility. It's more politically correct than "loony bin".'

Two snarled, 'Fuck politically correct.'

'What rats in the pipes?' I asked. It was then that something screamed inside me. Inexplicable fear came to me. My stomach lurched and my skin broke out in prickling gooseflesh. I felt nauseous and thought I was going to vomit. I summoned every fibre of my being to maintain my cool exterior. They weren't who they said they were. Then again, who did they say they were? Upholders of justice, named One and Two? Hello, but what does that even mean?

Two added, 'Copper.'

'Copper what?' asked One.

'The shit pipes,' Two prompted. 'They're made of copper.'

One snapped. 'Who cares if they're made from fucking marshmallows?! Can we just get this over with?'

Disgruntled, Two murmured, 'Marshmallows? That won't work. Yucky!'

Yucky? The flesh on the nape of my neck crawled.

I heard the very same word through my headset at the 112 call centre. It isn't so remarkable to hear the same word twice in the same week, but a word like yucky?

Staring at me, One asked, 'How long have you been in here?'

'Shouldn't you know that?'

'Just answer the question, Janey. How long have you been here?'

'Since I got the call at the 112 centre where I work. That's where I had my breakdown — those poor, poor children. I don't know what came over me. They're haunting me. Every time I blink, I see them in that nanosecond of darkness. At night, they come to my bed and lie with me.'

One and Two smiled at me.

And so I told my story, honestly and truthfully, for the first time in my life…

'I was a danger to myself and society. My unhinged mind had been festering for months. The accident took my husband and children, leaving me in a state of overwhelming grief that held my mind, body, and spirit hostage. By the time I found myself gravitating towards the playground of the local orphanage, I had given in to my burgeoning madness. I watched the children from a safe distance. I cannot describe how much I wanted to take two of those children home and keep them as my own and give them a loving home. I needed to fill the gap left in the house in the absence of my children. Call it a motherly need. I don't know. All I knew was that I craved a little boy and a girl, see. But this time, I would never let them go.'

One and Two exchanged glances.

'It wasn't too difficult to lure the boy and girl away from the playground. I studied that group of children every day for six weeks, how they would go to the public park with their minders. They followed the same routine every day. I found a weakness…I won't tell you what that weakness was. Then I lured them to my car with some misdirection. Without ever knowing they were hostages, nine-year-old and seven-year-old James and Megan came to live with me on the outskirts of town. They lived inside the house and were never let outside — especially when the police called to the house asking if I had seen anything unusual. I homeschooled them.' I paused as that old anxiety came into my padded cell light a draught from under the door. 'But the fear crept back.'

Two interrupted, 'Fear?'

'The fear of losing my children for a second time. There was only one way I knew how to keep them forever.'

I noticed how Two shifted uneasily while his accomplice's eyes became deep hallucinogenic pools in which I was drowning. 'Go on…' she softly encouraged.

I willed myself to go on. 'Little by little, I poisoned them with ricin I made myself with castor beans from my castor bean plant growing in the back garden.'

One's eyes were swirling now, and she sounded a

little wheezy when she spoke. 'Home produce? You must be proud.'

'I gave the boy and girl tiny doses. They didn't suffer in the end, just breathlessness, low blood pressure, and dehydration. I intended to accompany them on their journey to the promised land where we could live forever. I swallowed enough castor bean poison to put out a piebald stallion in one go, but for some reason, the poison didn't kill me. Mama always told me I had a tough constitution. It was agony. Hours and hours of writhing in pain next to the dead bodies of my children.'

'Poor thing. It must have been awful,' said Two with more than a hint of sarcasm.

'Maybe it was their way of getting back at you?' One was struggling with her breathing.

'The thought crossed my mind.' I gestured to the left side of my face. 'The ricin caused this horrible disfigurement. I call it my deathmark.'

'As opposed to your birthmark?' Two's tic was getting worse. He was losing control of his facial muscles, twitching and spasming. I wondered at what point should I ask him if he was feeling okay. 'My deathmark is my constant reminder.'

One laboured through her question. 'And then what did you do?'

'I buried them in the crawl space. As time went on, I felt better about having my children in the ground. It was peace of mind having them in the foundations of the house. I had control. They were safe with me.' I sighed.

'That's one way of putting it,' said Two with a mean grin.

I went on. 'But they haunted me. I may have buried them underground, but they're still in the house, haunting me. I know it's only my addled brain haunting me. I tried to get on with my life, happy in the knowing I had them forever, but the guilt gnawed at me while I slept. I took a job at 112 in the hope I might redeem myself by saving other lives.'

'And did that work?' asked Two.

I shook my head. 'That's when the bad dreams became reality. I thought it was a crank call when they — I — called me. I called myself because I'm insane. My conscience was on the other end of that line.'

Silence filled the room.

'They always know when to come and visit.'

One asked, 'And when is that?'

'When I'm asleep.'

Two asked, 'Why is that?'

There was something about the inflexion in his voice that told me he knew why. 'Cos that's when I'm at my most vulnerable. Those whispering voices telling me they will come to collect. They said I would know it was them because they would knock once. Not on my front door, but on the underside of my bed.' Something came to me just then. 'They pushed me to this, see? I think I could have gone on living for my remaining years with my dirty secret. They knew they would scare me into confessing. They got their death wish.'

'And revenge,' said Two, smacking his lips, 'is a dish best served cold.'

They stared at me, all stone cold.

With a horrible grimace, Two asked, 'What did they say to you?'

I told him what the children said. My skin crept when I realised that the detective sitting on my bed was lip-synching my words like a terrible actor — the words used by the children, to be more precise. I sweat all over again, and I thought I was going to throw up. What was happening here?

Two broke the silence in the padded cell. 'Now their little bodies are buried by the sewer pipes.'

One held me in her hypnotic stare. 'Yucky!'

There's that word again. 'Why are you saying that?'

'What?' wheezed One. 'Isn't it yucky? Knowing that you're buried under a house by stinking sewer pipes? Isn't it a yucky insult to be buried amongst shit pipes? It's symbolic, don't you think?'

They're trying to fuck with my head.

Two said, 'We analysed the material. It wasn't your imagination, Janey.'

'What do you mean?' *This isn't happening...*

One continued. 'Those two children you were raving about when the authorities brought you here were recorded, right up...'

'No! I don't believe you!'

'...until the moment you pulled the headset off your head. And even then, they kept crying out for help. But nobody would listen.'

'That's not true. Yes, they are driving me crazy. But it's my crazy. They don't exist. It's all in my head!'

'Well, now it's all in your headset,' smiled the woman as she stroked my hair. She then reached into her pocket and pulled out a tiny tape recorder that looked as if it was from the 1970s. She pressed play and held the little device up in front of me…and I almost fainted when those muted children's voices came from the fog of white noise. They were crying and pleading to be found and let out. I screamed, and I screamed again on hearing those words. My world was crashing down around me. This made little sense. I was sure they were calling my bluff, yet I heard those same voices and words.

'Your workmate, Sonia?' Two inquired.

I just about nodded.

'She heard the children on your headset. And one other individual whose name escapes me now.'

'There's no need to lie! My imagination is my purgatory. There is no more that you can say or do to make this any worse. Those voices may as well be real.'

'But they are real,' said One.

I screamed on cue. 'They're not real! I did something terrible and I'm paying the price. I know what I've done!'

One replayed the recording. This time, the static was gone from the audio and the children's voices pleaded from the speaker:

'Pleeease, help us! We're just children…'

'Switch it off!' I cried. But those haunted words crackled from the speaker. Then came their haunting chant:

'The Widow Slater… The Widow Slater… The Widow Slater…'

One and Two joined in the strange mantra, their voices growing louder and louder until they were screaming in my face.

I closed my eyes and blocked my ears. 'You're not real!' I screamed to counteract the piercing mantra. 'You're not real! … You're not real! … You're not…!' But when I opened my eyes, I wished I hadn't. Two's face was morphing into the grimacing face of the boy whom I poisoned, James. He fell to the floor in a writhing heap.

And now I knew there was nobody in my room. These two strangers were just another product of my guilt-riddled brain. My creations were more terrifying than anything that could have come back from the shallow grave because it was me frightening the living daylights out of myself, conjuring up these hair-raising hallucinations!

Now, Two's tongue came from his mouth. He smacked at his lips like before, as if he'd just found a tasty bacon morsel lodged in his teeth. But I knew now, as the chickens were coming home to roost (only they weren't chickens), that tongue-flicking was in search of water to quench his agonising thirst. I had seen that same thirsty gesture at the dinner table as the ricin took hold of the boy's system, with manic lip-licking. Oh, the thoughts of it! And One was on the floor, dragging herself around in circles, clawing at—

'Get me the fuck outta here!' I bawled into the camera in the ceiling corner, frantically waving to be seen by one of the security guards.

—her neck, gulping at the air like a landed sea salmon. That faint asthma wheezing I'd heard from her had graduated into red-faced retching gulps…

They mouldered away, but something came from their sloughed skins. Children's cries replaced the adult groans and moans of this nightmare. Child-ghost banshee wailing came spinning around my room at The Hillside at blurring speed, screaming round and around…

Two shadows skittered across the floor from those sloughed adult skins, moving towards the toilet. Then I heard them calling me from the toilet cubicle, calling me with their distressed little voices. James and Megan were in there. Oh, Jesus, the children were in the toilet of dreams!

Wake the fuck up, Janey! This is all just one baaad dream! They don't exist! They are dead and buried, nestled amongst the pipes, right below your en-suite bathroom toilet…

'Momma-Jane! Momma-Jane! Help!'

The voices came in perfect unison. Oh dear Jesus in Heaven, but it ripped my heart in two to hear their little voices again. They used to call me Momma-Jane!

But now, between those frantic Momma-Jane pleas came the splashing and bubbling of water. I fell from my bed, crawled to the cubicle, and fell against the toilet bowl from where the garbled voices were coming and I squinted into the water to see their faces peering up at me from down inside the U-bend. But how…?

'Jenny is down here with us, Momma-Jane…' Megan bubbled.

James gargled, 'And Noel too! We're best friends down here, Momma-Jane! We're happy in the toilet.'

A helpless whimper escaped my lips on hearing my children's names — my *real* children's names.

'Mommy? Look, it's me. It's me, Jenny. I'm in the toilet.' A childish giggle came up out of the bowl. Another titter joined Megan. 'I'm Noel, Mommy. Do you remember my voice?'

I lost all reason when I heard their voices. 'Jennifer? Noel? What are you doing down there?' Jennifer and Noel were taken from me in a freak boating accident. They died in water and here they were now, still in the water. It made strange sense. Yes! All my children were living in the U-bend of my —

'Mommy, we want to get out. Help us?' came Noel and Jennifer's fizzing voices.

'Yeah, Momma-Jane. Help us out…'

I bent over to find their faces in the water…

Four flesh-flapping, decaying little arms darted

from the water.

'Huh?' was all I had time to utter before those splashing pallid hands grabbed me and pulled me down head-first into the—

*

The two security guards were sitting in their little office in the bowels of The Hillside. One of them was a haggard individual who had served his fair share of time as a security guard at the psychiatric facility, but the other clean-shaven man was new and in training.

'Slater's having another episode,' said the older individual. 'Crazy as a broom handle. Ever seen a crazy broom handle, O'Connor?'

O'Connor had to think about that. 'No, I haven't. Who is Slater?' asked the newcomer.

'Janey Slater. The press is calling her Black Widow Slater. She killed a couple of kids — orphans from the orphanage. Would you believe it? She lost her own kids in some boating accident. They drowned along with her husband. It was all very tragic. Slater never got over it and just disintegrated into madness. In a way, I feel sorry for the poor old bitch. She kidnapped two kids from the orphanage and, somehow,' he shook his head, 'convinced herself that they were her own kids.'

'What happened?'

'She poisoned 'em. Little by little, she ended their lives. She was slipping them minute doses of ricin with their meals. She would have got away with it, only the town hall was, is, laying new fibre-optic cable…internet stuff.'

'5G?'

'Jesus, O'Connor, 3G's...7G's! What do I know? But what I know is that they found their bodies near the foundations of the house last week. They gave their little skeletons a decent burial — if such a thing exists. The state pathologist says they were down there next to the sewer pipes for the best part of five years. The discovery of the bodies coincides with Slater's mental break. Maths was never my strong point, but it seems The Widow heard those kids on her headset at the 112 call centre out there in the industrial estate about the same time they found the bodies.' He sighed wearily. 'I'm not someone for the supernatural,' pronouncing it as super natural, 'but it wouldn't surprise me if their spirits were freed when that road crew put a hole in the ground. Ghosts, O'Connor.'

'Huh?' O'Connor looked about him.

Another long sigh. 'Is it any wonder I want to retire early? Hmm? Seeing these sad excuses for human beings — the criminally insane — have taken all the wind outta my sails, son.' He huffed a tired chuckle. 'And I was thinking about buying a boat for my retirement.'

O'Connor mumbled, 'Ironic.'

The old hand considered his assistant, impressed with O'Connor's sly observation. 'Ironic? Yes. That's the word I was looking for.'

The young security guard gulped as he watched the crazed woman on the camera, waving her arms, screaming something about people in her room who shouldn't be there. 'Shouldn't we alert the nurses or something?'

'Son, she's been having these psychotic episodes every day for the last seven days, screaming blue murder about the ghosts that haunt her, pardon the unfortunate pun. I guess the guilt of what she did has finally caught up with her. Loopy,' was the security guard's diagnosis. 'Maybe we'll just let her stew for a while.' The old security guard watched the monitor where Janey Slater screamed in black and white silence with a certain relish etched on his face. 'Those poor kids,' he said to himself and anyone else who cared to listen.

O'Connor pointed at the screen. 'What's that?'

'What?' The old dog donned his spectacles and stared at the screen. 'I see nothing.'

'There's something happening off-camera'. The new security guard showed where he suspected something just happened below the angle of the camera. He deduced this by following the line of Slater's crazed eyes.

'There's nothing there,' said the other man.

'As God is my witness, I just saw two shadows cross that floor and go into the toilet cubicle.'

'I think you might have smoked the ole' devil's lettuce before you started your shift, O'Connor. Besides,' he raised his bushy eyebrows, 'look at the state of the world. You'll need a stronger witness.'

They watched Janey Slater argue with nobody, fall off her bed, then crawl like an animal through the toilet cubicle door. They waited, and then they waited

110

some more, but Janey Slater aka The Black Widow never came back. O'Connor asked his boss if they should go and, '…inspect her or something?'

The old hand checked his wristwatch. 'We'll give her another few minutes. Ole' Janey needs to do some major soul searching.'

Dead End

Dead-Ends 6

Bad Blood

I

Baby Starkweather was born prematurely on a snowy Halloween night in a little thatch cottage on the side of a steep hill known locally as Buck's Hill. There was a lot of blood. With so much blood, the infant Starkweather's mother didn't make it through the birth. Midwife Shelly was left with a gushing haemorrhage she couldn't control. She'd always wondered why the unassuming but brave midwife stepped into the scene on TV and demanded, 'Warm water and towels'. She had never understood that until the bloodiest Halloween night in history. There was so much of the red stuff that the newborn almost drowned in it.

In time, some would say Baby Starkweather drowned in blood, and the result resembled what occurs when babies are deprived of oxygen for more than five minutes…but not exactly.

In reality, Shelly wasn't a midwife at all, but the baby's aunt. The Starkweather sisters worked in the office at the sawmill down the hill. A blanket of snow covered the landscape on that October 31st night and the only road off the windswept mountain was a glassy sheet of black ice. They had no choice but to opt for a home birth, which caught the Starkweather sisters by surprise. On top of that was the strange fact that Shelly's sister's pregnancy lasted half the normal nine-month gestation period. But perhaps the biggest mystery was the baby's father. Her sister never revealed who the baby's father was, suffice to say that he came in the night, ahem, and absconded into the same night. It was as if her sister had left her bedroom window open for her romantic interest. This was irregular because the sisters lived under the same thatched roof and lived alone. They were known as The Nuns in town for the love of God. That said a lot in a place like Old Castle.

Once distraught Shelly Starkweather called the relevant authorities, she swaddled the newborn in a warm blanket and gripped him. Her eyes darted between the infant's deathly pale face in the glow of the open fire in the living room and his dead mother lying on the bloodied sheep's wool rug in front of the fireplace. Shelly's eyes rested on those vast crimson stains on the white rug. That image had a peculiar effect on her and all she could think about was her sister's blood soaking into the roots of the wool rug that had come from a skinned slaughtered sheep which had donated its flesh, wool, and entire tasty mutton carcass. But most of all, Shelly Starkweather wondered about this little mystery bundle. She racked her brain, trying to decipher who the father was. Whoever he was, he had obligations now. Shelly went through fifteen suitors in town, but couldn't decide on any of them for sure. Her sister had not given her any clue who she might have been liaising with. The baby's aunt thought back to the first time she noticed when her sister started 'to show'. That slight swelling in the tummy area and avoiding drinking their normal tipple of rum before bedtime. Yes, she recalled the night her sister had refused the nightcap. That was the same August weekend she heard odd sounds coming through the straw roof, sounding like someone walking across her ceiling in the middle of the night. Shelly slept in the attic, right beneath the thatched roof. She put it down to a strange dream and never recalled it until now as she watched Baby Starkweather suck on her bloody thumb.

Shelly gagged and took the child to be washed. As she crossed to the kitchen sink and filled a pot of water, she saw how Baby Starkweather sniffed at his little hand, and how his tiny pale tongue darted from his mouth and licked the blood from his fingers. He enjoyed blood, and it turned his aunt's stomach. There was some consolation in knowing that it was just a baby and that's what babies do…suck their fingers. Only, Baby Starkweather relished the plasma, nutrients, red and white cells, and platelets. Little Starkweather smacked his lips and his nostrils pulsed. It sickened Shelly to see how his dead mother's blood — her sister's lifeblood — had turned his tongue red as if the infant Starkweather was sucking on a strawberry lollipop.

But over the coming hours, Shelly realised there was something very odd about Baby Starkweather. She didn't have any baby experience, but she had her female gut instinct, and she didn't like what her gut was whispering to her.

Shelly Starkweather formally adopted her sister's baby. She felt she owed it to the child. Other than the normal reasons for wanting to adopt the baby, Shelly felt guilt-ridden for having her sister die on her watch and leaving the child without a mother. She could make up for it by taking the child under her wing.

But an issue soon manifested; the child refused to drink from his bottle of formula milk. Shelly tried everything. She took him to the family GP, who was of no help, then to expensive experts in the city. All to no avail. She even bought a latex breast filled with formula milk and became the surrogate mother she never wanted to be. But the baby was wasting away before her eyes. She was desperate to keep him alive and would do anything. Shelly had let her sister die, but she wouldn't let her baby die.

Shelly took her nephew (now her son) to Limerick City Hospital, where they put the month-old baby on a drip through which they fed the child. It ripped at her heart to see how the clumsy nurses couldn't find a 'good vein' to insert the drip line. The baby screamed with every failed attempt. Tears came to Shelly's eyes, and she had to turn away, but that only made it worse. But something odd happened during those horrid moments while the incompetent staff used Baby Starkweather as a human pin-cushion. In the struggle to find a 'good vein' in the baby's tiny arm, the amateur paediatric nurses wiped up the blood droplets in a gauze and left the bloody gauze on the bed by the baby's head. The three bloodied gauzes had a strange effect on the tiny tot. In the struggle to find the much coveted good vein, the hospital staff didn't see how the infant's nostrils flexed and his head turned in the blood's direction. Baby Starkweather's tropical sea-blue eyes searched for the source of that scent. Shelly was sure the nurses didn't notice how his little noggin inched towards the bloodied gauze and his pink tongue darted in and out from the corner of his mouth in a reptilian fashion.

The nurses found a 'good vein' and drip-fed Baby Starkweather through an IV line.

But by ten o'clock that night, the baby was on a life-support machine. The infant had an adverse reaction to his intravenous food. The staff couldn't understand it. The baby screamed and broke out in a terrible rash, red and raw like a birthmark. Baby Starkweather had an adverse reaction to everything and anything, including calories, proteins, fats, and electrolytes, including sodium, potassium, chloride, magnesium, and calcium. The paediatric nurses told this to Shelly, word for word, but Shelly was thinking about how the nurses cleared away those bloody gauzes and the infant's striking eyes followed the staff with pinpoint accuracy as they left the ward, sniffing at the bloody trail they left behind them…

She couldn't just watch him wither away like that in the little cot. She picked him up and held him in her arms. He weighed nothing. The foster mother could've been holding a bunch of rags in a baby-grow. Shelly Starkweather remembered the night the infant sucked the blood from his thumb and how he licked his lips. Sitting there in the paediatric ward, she had a light bulb moment — a pretty twisted light bulb moment, to be fair. She searched her handbag, but there was nothing sharp or pointy enough to do the job. Then she looked about the room for a suitable tool. Nope, nothing there. Shelly left the ward and went downstairs to the café, where she scanned the counter for a suitable implement to do the job. All she needed was something with a small pointed tip, enough to pierce the skin. She spotted a plastic jar of toothpicks by the cash register. She was about to ask for one when she decided it was a bad idea. She wasn't sure if a toothpick was sharp enough to pierce her skin. But more worryingly, what if the tip of the toothpick broke off in her flesh? Having a wood splinter stuck in her skin was no joke and it could cause an infection. No, that wouldn't work. Shelly scanned the hospital café again. She was about to give up hope when she saw a 'Missing Cat' poster pinned to a noticeboard over by the display case containing jam doughnuts and other yummy offerings. Cute cat, but it was more about the thumbtacks pinning the poster. She sidled up to the noticeboard and plucked one tack from the cork board, then went upstairs. Halfway up the stairs, an icy prickle of fear crept over her. Shelly felt the sudden urge to bound up those stairs. As she approached the tiny cot in the ward, her heart fluttered at seeing the baby, so small and insignificant she could hardly see him. The infant had turned a lighter shade of pale and looked too still for

117

Shelly's liking. A sob clutched in her throat. She reached down and picked him up. He was limp, but breathing. She panicked and was about to scream for help when she remembered the reason she had gone down to the café. Holding the baby in her left arm, she searched her right pocket for the thumbtack. It was in there and she bloody well knew it because it was pinching her. She had shoved it in there without thinking when she saw the state of the child. Shelly sat on the uncomfortable plastic chair with her adopted son in her arms. Taking a cautious glance about the quiet ward in relative darkness, she pricked the tip of the small finger of her right hand. She winced in pain as she squeezed the blood from the wound and watched the droplets of blood appear at the tip of her pinkie and fill out. No sooner had the blood bloomed when Baby Starkweather showed signs of life, turning in his blanket in the direction of Shelly's finger, by God. It was amazing and terrifying to witness. She dabbed the forefinger of her right hand onto the crimson droplet and, taking another glance around, rubbed her finger on the baby's lips…

Shelly's blood had the effect of smelling salts on the infant. Little Starkweather suckled at thin air as if slurping from an invisible bottle of milk. Heart pounding, Shelly dabbed the child's lips on the red stuff and the little guy turned ravenous. He took Shelly's small finger in both of his miniature hands like a squirrel clutching a hazelnut and guided her finger into his mouth and sucked just like any baby on instinct…and sucked…and sucked until Shelly's

118

finger throbbed as the baby siphoned his blood donor.

It wasn't long before a group of nurses and doctors gathered at young Starkweather's bedside, watching how the infant sucked on Shelly's little finger. The loud smack of minute lips filled this corner of the hospital room. They thought it was hilarious and awe-inspiring how the baby had made such a turnaround, not because the baby was drinking blood right before their eyes. They took pride in their work, nodding approvingly. Shelly smiled back and kept her pinky finger in the young child's mouth. Not that she had any choice. The child latched onto her like a tic.

The next morning, Baby Starkweather looked healthy, with rosy cheeks and a full belly. Like a vampire bat, the infant satisfied his hunger with his adoptive mother's blood during the night.

When the nurses and doctors approached the Starkweather cot on their rounds, they couldn't believe the improvement the baby had made overnight. But the mother's deterioration equally startled them.

'Are you okay?' asked one nurse. 'You look a little peaky.'

'That's one way of putting it,' said her colleague, the same nurse who had made various failed attempts at finding '…a good vein'. 'She looks half dead.'

'I have slept little,' said Shelly, feeling as weak as she looked.

'You need to get some sugar into you, my dear,' said the third nurse.

And blood maybe? Shelly thought.

Pin-Cushion suggested, 'Why don't you take yourself down to the café and get yourself a mug of coffee and one of those delicious custard slices? Hmm? It'll do you the world of good.'

Her younger colleague added with a chortle, 'I was getting too fond of them. You'll find them in the display case over by the—'

'Noticeboard,' Shelly finished in a weak tone. 'Yes, I saw them. They look tasty.'

They smiled at the babe-in-arms suckling on Shelly's finger without knowing the infant was literally sucking the life out of his foster mother in front of them. His belly had tripled in size. Shelly didn't want the health professionals to see Baby Starkweather's distended tummy because that would lead to all kinds of awkward questions and answers. When one nurse went to take the child from her to allow her to go downstairs and eat, Shelly asked if it would be possible to do it a little later, as the infant was settled. They paused before agreeing. God knows, but nobody ever said being a mother was easy.

By now, she knew there was something very wrong with Baby Starkweather, but Shelly pledged she would save the oddity's life; she wasn't prepared to lose her sister and her sister's baby. She just wanted to bring the infant back from the dead, that's all. Then Shelly would face whatever she needed to face in life.

Knowing the hospital professionals did not know what they were dealing with, Shelly discharged the baby against the wishes of the hospital.

II

By the time Baby Starkweather celebrated his 3rd birthday, Shelly Starkweather had grown old prematurely, taking on the aspect of an advanced substance addict, shrivelled and waned. And she had the track marks to show it, only they were *teeth* marks. The toddler had formidable baby teeth or milk teeth, as they were called in an average normal household, but the Starkweather thatched cottage was anything but normal. No, this boy had blood teeth. The child had the mouth and jaws of a piranha fish. Shelly Starkweather did everything to keep the toddler in blood. But she had reached the end of her tether. She couldn't keep up with the child's voracious feeding times. Baby Starkweather was draining her, not only of blood, but her energy, too. The child's adoptive mother kept donating blood but didn't have enough time to generate new red stuff. She was fighting a losing battle and floated about the sawmill office every day as if she were the living dead. It was time to find other ways of feeding Baby Starkweather.

Shelly Starkweather started working two jobs to provide for her child, and became a criminal, resorting to robbing a bank. But not any old bank…

the blood bank. She went down to the local blood bank one day in Old Castle to enquire about donating blood. The last thing on her mind was donating blood — she didn't have enough of the damn stuff. In her gross innocence, Shelly intended to find a few bags of blood lying around. What did she think it was? An abattoir? Or a blood sausage factory? Miss Starkweather was misguided. But providence was on Shelly's side that Tuesday evening. Shelly Starkweather was an amiable woman, see, and picked up friends with ease. It wasn't long before the bank secretary was offering part-time evening work to Shelly. And whoever said God doesn't work in mysterious ways?

'What would my role be?' asked Shelly, getting very excited.

'Collecting the blood in plastic pouches.'

Yes, what strange gods were looking down on Shelly Starkweather and her freak baby?

The blood bank secretary continued speaking to Shelly, filling her in on what her duties would be, but all the adoptive mother could see was a pool of blood and her li'l cutie doing the backstroke in this flowing swimming pool of crimson.

It was a two-hour shift from 6 pm to 8 pm Monday to Friday. Shelly hired a childminder for the two hours every evening with the strict instructions that she shouldn't offer the child anything to eat, citing '…a strange allergy to various foods,' as the reason.

By day, Shelly Starkweather worked with pints of

donated blood, and by night, she stole those pints. One night, a security guard got suspicious when Shelly left the clinic looking fatter than when she went in just two hours previous. He had been spying on her for days before springing on her and asking to see under Shelly's top. Shelly obliged the security man, combining his work duties with a sneaky come-on. She was looking for a man in her life to share the burden, i.e., feeding Baby Starkweather.

'Blood? You're stealing blood?' he asked Shelly, looking under her top, finding five pints of blood strapped to her body. 'Am I missing something here?'

Larry, the security guard, had the hots for her. Shelly knew this, and she would use it to her advantage. 'I'm a sexy vampire and this is my suicide vest.' Timing was never Shelly's strong point.

Ill-timed or not, Larry couldn't get enough of quirky Shelly and her blood fetish. Using love to her advantage, Shelly Starkweather told Larry she would go out on a date with him *if* he kept the topic of the stolen blood to himself. She explained, 'It's a long story. I'll introduce you to him when you come round.'

'Who?'

'The long story.'

A strict routine of working by day, stealing by evening, and feeding by night took its toll on Shelly. One may ask why Shelly just didn't hand over the child to a specialist centre for daemonic babies. First, such a place didn't exist in the small town of Old Castle, with a population of 7,209. And she knew she would lose her baby and he would become a sideshow freak; a curiosity for the public.

During this period of her life, Shelly Starkweather often wished she could go down into her sister's grave and ask her about the secret she took to that grave. Who is the baby's father? Baby Starkweather had turned three years old, and no male in town had ever shown any extra interest in the toddler. He was a mystery baby from a mystery man.

III

Shelly Starkweather introduced the man in her life to 'the long story', aka Baby Starkweather.

What Larry saw (but failed to mention) was a cute little boy with a mouth that was a tad too wide for his face. He loved it when the toddler smiled at him, but sometimes the corners of that smile went right around to his earlobes and the security guard struggled to hold his return smile. The child had a wonderful head of flame-red curls, but a wan complexion and a dead stare that would be quite at home on death row. The baby had a pot belly, but Larry found that quite cute. The child was always looking at him, but he would turn away when the security guard caught his lifeless gaze. The child was a watcher. Jack knew about this class of humans through his work. Fair enough, he didn't see many watchers at the blood bank, but he'd seen them at previous work posts like at The Hillside Psychiatric Hospital out on the coast road. Sometimes, Larry wanted to know what the little guy was thinking about with the far-off dead headlights he called eyes, but on second thoughts, perhaps he didn't want to know.

A month later, the security guard moved into the thatched cottage on the Buck's Hill. He made it official by signing the paperwork to become the boy's legal guardian. That very evening, after signing all the relevant documentation, Larry asked Shelly to marry him.

'What?' Shelly startled while surreptitiously cleaning Baby's bloody face after supper — she still hadn't told Larry about his adopted son's strange diet. She wanted him in and settled before she broke that news.

'I would like your hand in marriage.'

Shelly lit up with delight and agreed, but only on the proviso: 'Only if you marry the rest of me, too, Lars.'

Larry loved Shelly's quirky sense of humour and bent over in a real gut-buster of laughter.

While he was bent over, Shelly took this succinct juncture to sidestep in front of Baby to block Larry's view of the child. His face and bib were smeared in the crimson stuff and she needed to come up with an answer to the conversation that was coming one of these days. That short and sweet conversation would go something like:

'What's up with the blood?'

'Don't be silly! That's not blood, Lars, that's ketchup. He loves the stuff!'

'Well, be careful because ketchup is full of sugar.'

To Shelly's amazement, the security guard had never asked her where all that stolen blood was going. She had spun him the story about blood sausage and how she loved to cook, but that would only stretch so far, especially when they never ate blood sausage. She decided she needed to sit down with Larry and break it to him gently. Shelly would tell him on Saturday night after she fed him enough alcohol to numb a horse.

When Saturday night arrived, Shelly Starkweather got her man liquored up on one cocktail she liked to invent when she was feeling foxy. On this night, she unleashed her Hairy Canary upon Larry. 'Fancy a Hairy Canary?'

Judging by the security guard's lit reaction, Shelly assumed Larry thought her invite was sexual. She clarified the situation. It might've been easier just to make some Bloody Marys, but Shelly had her fill of all things bloody, thank you very much.

Once Larry was rat-arsed on Hairy Canaries, Shelly revealed the truth about his adopted son. But instead of giving him a theory class, she opted for a practical class. She sat herself down by the open fire and before Larry knew what was happening, Shelly had made a quick and efficient incision on 'a good vein' in her left wrist.

Security guard, Larry, screamed, 'Jesus Christ above!' and ran to Shelly's side. She told him to relax and assured him that everything was okay. If '…

everything's okay,' meant a three-year-old boy smelling blood from the other side of the house and coming running to his mother with his jaw agape, resembling something only found in the murky depths of the Amazon river, then yes, everything was okay. The security guard fainted when he saw how the child latched onto his mama's wrist. When Larry came to, the first thing he saw was Shelly, flopped in the armchair, her deathly pale face aglow in the embers. There wasn't a sound in the kitchen except for the rhythmic sucking of the child siphoning blood from Shelly. Her arm hung over the armrest of the chair while the overgrown baby worked on her wrist. Baby Starkweather turned around to look at Larry with a devilishly gory grin. That was it for Larry. He was packing his bags until Shelly told him about the night the infant almost died at the intensive care unit in Limerick City Hospital. She told him how the doctors couldn't help him, but they could. He was alive because of Shelly, but she couldn't keep up the bloodletting. The security guard found himself in a tight spot and had some major soul-searching to do.

It wasn't long before a true abnormality of nature was living on the side of that normal hill, where Shelly and Larry offered themselves to Baby Starkweather nightly: one night on, one night off. Larry, wanting to be a doting father figure for the child, offering himself up to be gorged and glutted upon. He had grown very fond of the strange little boy and convinced himself to donate a pint or two of the red stuff. After all, he was working at the blood bank and people were coming in off the street every day of the week and donating blood to strangers. The least he could do was donate his blood to his adopted son; it was a noble cause.

They took turns, like night watch, only blood watch.

The years slipped by. Baby Starkweather turned six years old and was going to school. He was a normal child in every aspect of his education and progressed at the same rhythm as his peers. But he rarely, if ever, spoke, and that stare gave his teachers the heebie-jeebies. Baby's teachers recommended various tests to be done in a qualified centre. Shelly knew it was the genetic make-up of the boy and nothing to be troubled about. He never brought lunch to school. But he sat with his classmates in the schoolyard and enjoyed watching them eat their corned beef sandwiches. Or rather, he enjoyed them. The child didn't know why, but for some reason, their necks seemed very attractive while they ate their tasty morsels. Baby liked how their interior and exterior jugular veins popped from the taut skin of their smooth necks when they worked their jaws. The bluish lines running beneath the skin transfixed him, and he could almost smell the blood spurting through those canals.

Sometimes, Shelly would turn up at the school on her lunch break at the sawmill and spy on her adopted son through the fence running along the side of the schoolyard. At first, it was just so uplifting to see him playing hide-and-seek with his classmates. But as the weeks passed by and her surreptitious visits increased, she realised Baby was always the one doing the seeking and the other boys and girls were doing the hiding. And that was when Shelly realised the children were terrified of her adopted son.

It was also around now when Baby Starkweather outright refused to eat during daylight hours, preferring the sweet veil of darkness to glutton on his foster parents. Now, instead of a hearty breakfast, he would starve himself until nightfall, and then more than make up for his absent brekkies. Each night, Shelly Starkweather brought a piece of equipment from the blood donation clinic to allow for a pain-free extraction, and when she could, she would bring a pint or two while Larry watched out for her. It was a risk worth taking to give them a little relief from the razor teeth. Shelly set up a comfortable blood-letting station in the living room, establishing an IV line while they watched their favourite TV programme while the youngster feasted. Once engorged, the child (only he was never a child, who are we kidding here?) wiped the blood from his lips, slathering the red stuff across his chubby cheeks and falling into bed in a bloated trance. The happy though drained couple called it the blood diner clinic instead of the blood donor clinic. It was an in-joke only Shelly and Larry, soulmates and blood brothers on every level, would understand — this mingling of blood.

But a day came when Larry passed out at the blood

bank. When the company doctor revised the security guard, she told him he had next to no blood pressure, which was ironic considering he was working in… well, a blood bank. The doc wanted to know where all the security guard's blood had gone. She asked as if Larry had misplaced his blood somewhere. He couldn't tell the doctor, but this was a wake-up call, deciding there and then he'd had enough of the freaks on the hill. The little tic was going to finish him some night, one sup too many. Bye-bye, Larry. Such a noble, brave, and fucking stupid for having gone along with this lunacy. But that was when he made the grave mistake of telling Shelly he wanted to get out of the relationship. 'I married a bloodsucker!'

'Why would you say that, Lars? I'm not a—'

'The kid, Shelly! I married the kid! I give him everything, even my blood, dammit!'

Larry also told Shelly that he would go to the authorities because he couldn't have that little fiend on his conscience.

Only Larry didn't know then that there was only one way out of this relationship.

By dawn, Shelly Starkweather had put Larry in the potato patch. He'd always loved potatoes in their many eating forms and she thought he would be much happier down amongst the tubers. And that his corpse would provide vital humus and fertiliser for the tubers was a sort of born-again experience. Some day in the future, Larry would be reincarnated as a plate of mashed potato…or 'pandy', as his dear mother used

130

to call it. She called her little Larry '...a pandy-belly' as opposed to his freakish adopted son, who was a... blood-belly? Bloody-Belly? No. Just *no*. It was a fitting end for Larry in Shelly's brain, which had become unhinged and diabolical somewhere along the way.

Shelly, being a practical and desperate woman, decided Larry had to go to save her surrogate son. Larry knew too much. She knocked him out with the car jack and tied him to an armchair by the kitchen fireplace. Shelly took considerable comfort in the knowing that he hadn't died a painful death. Shelly convinced herself battering Larry to death with a car jack was a peaceful way to go. Her husband had died a noble death by feeding his adopted son, who sucked him dry as his light went out. Shelly Starkweather watched as the colour left the security guard's cheeks while he slipped into a coma, then slipped further down into death. As far as Shelly Starkweather was concerned, her husband died in his sleep. It was the best way to go. But ultimately, it was the six-year-old who took his life. That the security guard could offer one last meal to his surrogate son in death was indeed a righteous gesture...even if he had no choice. It was still an upstanding thing to do.

Once she had buried Larry amongst the potato drills, Shelly flopped to the ground in a sweaty, panting heap, surrounded by stalks. It was here in this reverie, hidden from the world, where Shelly Starkweather realised she had created a monster and that monster had to go.

With teary eyes, Shelly got Baby Starkweather ready for school, as she did every other morning. Considering what was ahead, she contemplated giving the little cannibal a day off school. Just so that they could be together and make their last day count. But she wanted to have everything ready — he would be hungry when he came home. The freak of nature would be looking for his din-dins.

While he was at school, Shelly Starkweather set up the blood-letting station. But this time, she added some additional elements. She had learnt from experience that the human body can do remarkable things when in mortal danger. She saw how Larry pulled the sofa across the living room in his attempt to escape Baby's nipping chompers and sucking leeches for lips. Oh, yes, Shelly had to pop Larry on the head a second time with the car jack, though she would still insist her husband died a peaceful death in the bosom of his loved ones…who loved him so much that they ate him.

Shelly had been drinking from a sneaky flagon of whiskey all morning at the sawmill, hoping she would be sufficiently numb when the time came. At 2 pm she left the sawmill and went to Saint Molua's school to collect the entity known as Baby and took him home to their little thatch cottage on the side of the hill known as Buck's Hill. It was a day like any other…until Baby saw the recent additions to the blood donation station. The shiny sets of handcuffs glinted in his dead eyes, each cuff locked onto objects which couldn't be moved when the time came. Yes, Shelly had created a monster, and the monster had to go because *she* was the monster! She had let this aberration of nature grow and flourish into something that should only exist in nightmares, and her life had become a nightmare. One might say she fed and nourished the problem. She was Frankenstein. Only Frankenstein's monster was a lovable and sympathetic creature, more humane than his master and creator. But Shelly couldn't say the same for Baby Starkweather, who wasn't lovable, sympathetic, or humane. He was a cold, slippery, blind thing found under a rock and only came alive near the red stuff. How had she not seen this until now? Jesus Christ in Heaven! Shelly was aware that the thing living in her house was a glorified mosquito and was just as happy feasting on Mommy as a stranger. Not only that, the youngster didn't possess an OFF switch when it came to knowing when he — the bloated leech — had a full belly. If left to its own devices, an engorged Baby Starkweather would eat himself to death.

Equipped with this mortal knowledge, Shelly Starkweather put her immortal plan into action.

Now was the moment while the blood creature was immersed in his maths homework at the kitchen table. It broke the sawmill worker's heart to see that the thing-child loved school and could be someone someday. But she also knew he could eat someone

133

someday; it was a question of when not if. Baby Starkweather was a perversion of nature and she needed to remind herself of that as she cut a discreet nick in her arm. As she sliced her flesh, she watched Baby stall, look up from his textbook, and stare off into space as the first tendrils of the crimson wafted below his hypersensitive nostrils. She sat in the armchair and strapped herself into the cuffs, one on each ankle and two more on her wrists. Once secured, she whistled to Baby. It spun away from the table and came running like a dog. That was the call she used to tell him din-dins was ready. She had flushed the handcuff keys down the toilet and Shelly Starkweather was no Houdini. There was no getting away now as Baby Starkweather came bounding on all fours…yes, it was something he did before feasting; falling back into his ancestral beginnings… not that Shelly knew who those ancestors were — she didn't even know who his father was for crying out loud!

Baby Starkweather homed in on the area of skin where Shelly had pricked herself. With fire in his eyes, the abnormality latched and sucked mechanically. It was a real downer in knowing that this would be the closest Shelly would come to motherhood and breastfeeding.

Once Baby was sucking deep and in that deeper trance he went into whilst feeding, Shelly produced the blade she'd nicked herself with and slashed a considerable gash on Baby's right wrist where he might have worn a wristwatch in another lifetime. As her life trickled away, she saw how the blood trickled from the freak's arm. That was her blood spurting from him onto the pockmarked linoleum. Baby was in such a feeding frenzy it hadn't even noticed when Shelly had cut a gash through him. This was the reality of the situation right here, right now.

As the minutes passed by, she grew weaker and weaker while watching the ravenous thing become swollen on her vital liquid. She saw the blood pour from its wrist. Once it had sucked her dry, it would go to work on its wrist. This was Shelly Starkweather's immortal plan and what a beautiful plan it was. She just needed to stay awake to witness her scheme come to fruition. Baby, a cannibal at heart, would eat himself to death like some animals do. What a perfect way to go. If Baby Starkweather could choose a way to die, surely it would be to forage on himself. It was the ultimate act of sacrifice, and even though Shelly had grown a profound hatred for the little abnormality, she hoped he would find his gods wherever he was going.

By the time the sun went down over Buck's Hill, Shelly Starkweather's blood pressure had also gone down dramatically. Her arms and legs were cold and her skin was clammy. She was confused and delirious, but not lost enough to know she had done the right thing. Baby Starkweather had sucked every drop of blood from her and she awaited the angel of death to accompany her to the next life…when ballooning Baby turned on himself for nourishment.

A muffled thud sounded on the thatched roof.

As her light went out, she tracked the footfalls over the snarling and sucking coming from Baby as he supped and siphoned on his arm. As Shelly slipped into the valley of death, she heard scratching and scraping on the wall as whatever was outside came down the guttering.

My angel of death?

No, it couldn't be. Those same strange sounds that Shelly heard during that August long since gone came back to her memory.

More irregular footsteps came right up to the back door. Through the frosted glass and the approaching mist of death, Shelly Starkweather saw a face peer through the window. That countenance gave Shelly such a shock that it stopped the clock inside her heart. But as she succumbed, the sawmill secretary realised she knew those lifeless eyes because Baby had the same eyes! And to her amazement that came all too late, Shelly Starkweather knew her sister had seen the same face, but she had made the mistake of letting it into her bedroom…and into her bed.

It disappeared from the window. She heard it crawl up the outside wall and scramble across the long-straw thatch. The thing was coming down the soot-tarred chimney, and now it crawled out of the fireplace. The dying coals didn't seem to make any impression on it. The stranger crossed the room from the chimney hearth and kissed Baby on the head before pulling him away from himself. Then Shelly slipped into a spiral as the unwanted guest, this abomination of unfathomable horror, helped himself to Baby Starkweather's wrist. Oh, dear Jesus in Heaven! It then latched onto her wound left by Baby's eager jaws. It was pure ecstasy, almost a sexual experience as the stranger with the sharp teeth and the pale, translucent face pumped blood back into her. In the low light thrown from the dying embers, Shelly saw he was handsome in an offbeat way and understood why her sister might have opened her window to let him in one balmy night in a moment of weakness.

A mingling of blood took place.

The tall and very dark stranger snapped open those handcuffs as if they were made in China.

Then everything faded to black…

Night had descended when Shelly Starkweather felt herself coming back from a much darker place without ever knowing how she had got there. As she came back to life, she witnessed father and son climb into the fireplace, and then crawl their way up the sooty chimney, scrambling up through the flue. She heard their feet shuffling on the thatch roof…and then there was nothing but the wind whistling around the eaves of the old cottage up there on Buck's Hill. She was moved to tears by it. Shelly was Frankenstein's monster; a woman with monstrous love pumping through her veins.

Dead End

Dead-Ends 7

The Taxi Driver

Nobody knew Eva Montgomery had a nut allergy until she was halfway through a slice of her birthday cake. None of her family noticed the nut allergy warning on the cake wrapping. Nobody noticed it because nobody ever reacted to nuts in the Montgomery household...until now. It happened while the happy-go-lucky six-year-old was trying to blow out the relighting candles. The trick candles fascinated the little girl and she must've been blowing out the six candles and watching them relight for fifteen minutes. Her family sat around the table with big smiles on their faces, watching her struggle with the fizzling candles when she turned redder in the face than she had already been as she huffed and puffed. That was when the smiles dropped. A rash broke out on Eva's face and her family noticed how she began to gulp and swallow, like a fish out of water. The hilarity dried up when they realised Eva wasn't struggling with the magic candles but experiencing the onset of anaphylaxis. The sudden shock on her face in the light of the joke candles stopped hearts.

Eva's father, Jake, glanced at his wife, Rachel. In that panicked exchange, they both knew they had a serious issue on their hands. On any other night of the week, they would park their car in the community car park under the building, but it was at the mechanics for a service. Jake serviced his car once every year and sometimes left it for two years. Murphy's law. Well, fuck Murphy and his law!

In her blind panic, Eva's mother screamed on cue, 'Call an ambulance!' Hoping someone was already on the phone with the emergency services. When she saw that everyone else was in hysteria around the suffocating child, she pulled her phone from her back pocket and keyed in 112. Within seconds, she was screaming down the line, pleading for an ambulance to come to their flat on Henry Street, please.

Jake held his head in his hands, walking around in circles, unsure whether to wait for an ambulance or go down to the street and find a taxi. 'Fuck! Fuck! Fuck!' he roared over and over again.

And now there was another cold front coming in on this very night to create the perfect storm. The annual food festival was on in the city and many streets were closed off. Jake deduced he needed to be on the street. He would take the first form of transport he found. If that meant robbing a child's tricycle and sitting Eva in the basket, then so be it.

'We don't have time!' Rachel cried. 'The ambulance is on its way, but it's stuck in traffic on the other side of the city!'

'Get her ready!' Jake bawled at his wife. 'I'm taking her down to the street and I'll hijack the first car I see!' He turned to his older daughter, Charlotte, and ordered her to get Eva's boots and coat on. But the 12-year-old girl had gone into shutdown and insisted on asking her mother and father what the matter was with her sister: 'What's wrong with Eva?'

Jake pulled on his boots and jacket as it was a freezing night. He slammed the door behind him, listening to his wife on the phone with the ambulance staff. 'We don't have time! Tell them I'm going down to the street with her! Maybe I can meet them on the way. If not, I'll stop someone!'

As he shut the door behind him, he heard Rachel asking the medics their whereabouts. 'They're at the top of O'Connell Street, making their way to Henry Street,' she called back to him.

'Jesus Christ,' yelled Jake. 'It's going to take them at least twenty minutes to get here! She's choking!'

Jake saw how Eva was turning purple as her throat restricted and narrowed. Her hitching breaths cast a claustrophobic net over him. Eva's mother told him she would come too and bring Charlotte, but Jake told them to stay in the flat. There was nothing they could do and they would only freeze. That wasn't helping anyone. With reluctance, Eva's mother agreed to stay behind and watch Charlotte, and it was the most difficult thing she'd ever had to do.

Jake took the lift down to the ground floor and trundled out into the foyer with Eva in his arms. He was struggling to open the front door of the building when someone opened it for him. 'Cha?'

'You need my help,' the 12-year-old protested.

'Go back up to Mommy, Charlotte!'

140

But the 12-year-old, who had snuck out and stole down the stairs behind her father and sister, was having none of it. 'I'm coming with you. She's my sister. I can help!'

Jake didn't want to argue. He held Eva in his arms, whispering to her, 'Everything's going to be okay! Okay, Eva? Okay?!' He yelled, looking for a reaction from the child. She nodded. He took deep breaths, listening to his daughter's laboured breathing. It was as if Jake was breathing for his daughter. He whimpered a cursing tirade as he made his way down the steps to the street, never feeling more alone or useless in all his life. His 12-year-old daughter went down ahead of him, telling him the safest way down the steps through the patches of black ice. Strike that. He didn't feel alone, but he felt just as useless.

'The ambulance is on the way!' called Rachel through a window from a few floors above them. But the traffic was at a standstill. It might've been on its way, but Eva didn't have time. The streets were chock-a-block with people and cars.

'I can see the ambulance!' Eva's mother called.

Off in the distance, Jake and Charlotte heard the squawk of the ambulance.

Rachel added from above, 'But it's blocked in! There's a traffic jam up to the top of the street, Jake! What'll we do?!'

Desperate, Jake screamed up, 'I don't know what to do!'

The wail of a siren in the distance sounded again. It was too far off for Jake's liking. Eva's eyes were puffing out from their sockets while she tried to get oxygen into her lungs in sharp, ragged breaths.

Just when Jake thought he was going to pass out with adrenaline and nausea, a taxi pulled up to the curb. Jake and his daughter exchanged an incredulous glance when the back door popped open. Jake peered into the dark interior of the taxi. He clocked the silhouette behind the steering wheel. 'City Hospital! A&E!' he cried.

No answer came from the driver.

They jumped in.

'Please, hurry! My daughter's having an allergic reaction to something she ate.'

The driver didn't respond. He wasn't the talkative type, and that suited Jake just fine.

For now, how this miraculous taxi should pull up in front of them would remain a mystery.

Jake noticed how the driver kept looking forward, but eyed them in the rearview mirror. His searing eyes rested on little Eva sitting between Jake and Charlotte, puce and clawing at her throat. Jake struggled to keep a hold of her slippery hands as her fingernails tore at her neck. 'H-How are you going to get through all this traffic?' Jake asked, intrigued. If an ambulance with a screaming siren and swirling blue lights couldn't break through the blocked traffic, then how would a taxi—

The driver slammed on the accelerator. The taxi peeled away from the kerb, leaving two streaks of acrid-smelling burnt rubber on the street as a memory of what once was. In the gloomy light of the taxi's interior, all Jake could see was the driver's black frame at the wheel and those eyes staring back at him. They dove in and out of traffic. To Jake's amazement, the faster he gunned the taxi, the faster he could swerve in and out of oncoming vehicles. The real horror was becoming less about his six-year-old's nut allergy and more about those dark rearview eyes that never left distressed Eva Montgomery and rarely, if ever, watched the street ahead. It was like watching some actor driving along in a middle-of-the-road (literally) TV series while he looked at his passenger for far too long to be realistic. A thought crossed Jake's mind. He considered the driver might be deaf. That would explain his reticence to speak and fuel the reason he was gaping at them in the rearview mirror. Jake put himself in the driver's position and concluded he would do the same if he needed to lip-read. But it was too dark inside the taxi to see anything of significance. Then the notion struck Jake that the driver might not control the English language as well as he controlled this taxi. He might struggle to understand, so preferred to say nothing instead. He had probably learned the hard way not to engage in conversation, as it only led to complications. If—

The taxi driver declared into the rearview mirror, 'I am the best taxi driver in the city!' His words were more for the girls' benefit than their father's. There was almost something juvenile in his cadence. He was proud to be the city's best taxi driver. But what that meant was open to interpretation.

Eva didn't respond. Charlotte flashed a

consolatory smile. Jake was tense now. The worm of worry wriggled in his belly because this shadow man was in charge of all their lives right now. It didn't help that he remained in virtual darkness, save for the low illumination glowing from the dashboard.

The driver took his hands off the wheel and slapped at his chest. 'I am the best taxi driver in the city!' He repeated in monotone, gravelly tones. Jake's heart skipped a beat on spotting this. He wanted to scream at the driver, but not only Eva's life was in his hands now. Jake didn't want to say or do anything to rock the boat — the taxi, in this case.

The driver slapped the dashboard and said, 'I promise you I will get that little girl to the hospital…'

In a shard of light coming from the headlights behind them, Jake caught the glisten of sweat on the driver's ivory-pale brow as he turned to his left. But it was his odd voice that gave Jake something to think about.

The taxi jolted. The Montgomerys were pushed back into their seats with the G-force. And before any of them knew what was happening, the taxi had somehow squeezed through the traffic ahead and was careening down Connolly Avenue towards Limerick City Hospital. Charlotte screamed while Jake held onto his daughters for dear life while they rocked from side to side as the deranged — deranged? — yes, the man had come unhinged somewhere along this brief journey. Then again, maybe he was already crazy when they had sat in! The taxi careened down towards the end of Connolly Avenue, showing complete disregard for human life...except for the six-year-old girl in the back seat, distracting even Eva from her smothering nut allergy. He had taken his promise to heart. The driver slammed his fist on the dashboard as they 'ate road' — a saying the locals might use. They screamed through the city as the taxi narrowly missed several obstacles, swerving in and out of traffic.

Keeping his eyes in the mirror, not on the blur of traffic and streets, he repeated, 'I am the best taxi driver in the city.' His voice was hollow, and it sounded the same as when they had sat in; zero difference in his cadence between parked up at the footpath and zooming in and out of traffic at quadruple the speed limit...

At this terrifying juncture, Jake Montgomery noticed the driver's identity badge on the dashboard. His belly fluttered when he saw the man sitting in the front seat was not the man in the photograph. The lighting was poor, but no amount of poor light would convince Jake that the driver was the same man in the identification badge. His mind raced along with the runaway taxi. With growing anxiety, Jake had almost forgotten why they were on this hellish ride. But Eva reminded him when she called out, 'I...can't...buh-breathe!'

Up ahead, the traffic lights turned from green to amber to...

RED.

Jake cried, 'Jesus, no!' Traffic was pulling out from the intersection at Cecil Street up ahead to their right. He went to grab his girls and shield them from the inevitable crash of metal that was coming… coming…coming…

'Get down!' He snatched at his girls and closed his eyes as the taxi screamed into high gear…

But that crash of metal never came.

Charlotte cried. Seeing the tears streaking down his 12-year-old's face was too much. 'Sir, slow down, please.' The last thing Jake thought he would do was ask the driver to slow down.

The man at the wheel wasn't listening. He switched on the radio and tuned into the classical music channel. *Vivaldi's Four Seasons — Spring* filled the taxi. His eyes flitted from the streets ahead to Eva in his rearview and back again to the lit city streets. Another change of gears and they were going so fast now that Jake felt as if they were going to take off and glide over the traffic.

Jake pleaded, 'Please, slow down.'

The manic driver turned up the classical piece another notch, just to drown out Jake's imploring voice while he cut corners and peeled rubber. The driver commandeered the taxi through the streets with a complete disregard for traffic lights; their colours were there to make them pretty. Charlotte was hiding her face in her hands, screaming to be let out.

By the time they screeched into Limerick City Hospital's A&E car park, Eva was unconscious and her sister was conscious but traumatised. Jake wasn't sure which was worse as he fell out of the taxi onto the tarmac and carried his six-year-old through the doors of the accident and emergency department. He was briefly aware that the taxi had parked in the ambulance docking bay. The driver couldn't have got them any closer to the main doors.

A helpful grey-haired woman met him at the information desk who directed one orderly milling about to escort Mr Montgomery and his daughters to the relevant section of the hospital. The doctors took Eva from Jake and told him to wait outside in the hallway with Charlotte. It all happened in a flurry. It ripped him in two to leave his little girl like that, but those were the rules. Once his six-year-old disappeared behind those swinging doors, a fainting wave overpowered Jake Montgomery. He backed up to the wall to steady himself before slipping to the floor where he held his face in his hands and bawled as that rushing wave brought the adrenaline and anxiety.

Father and daughter waited for thirty agonising minutes. In the back of Jake's mind, he thought about the taxi driver waiting outside to be paid. If—

One of the junior doctors came through the pair of flapping doors and told Jake, through her face mask, that his youngest daughter was going to be okay. They gave her an adrenaline antidote to reverse the anaphylactic shock, which was indeed caused by the innocent but deadly birthday carrot cake.

'How did you get here tonight with the commotion in the city?' she asked.

And so Jake Montgomery relayed their hair-raising story, which had brought them up to this point. He knew he was talking too much, but Jake talked too much when he was nervous. It wasn't until he got to '...the crazy taxi driver' that the doctor interrupted.

'Your daughter is alive thanks to that crazy taxi driver. You need to thank him. And give him a generous tip while you're at it.'

Jake agreed wholeheartedly. His chin trembled. At that moment, he would have transferred his life savings to that anonymous taxi driver hidden in the shadows. He thanked the doctor from the bottom of his heart and told her to pass on his sincerest thanks to the rest of the team.

Jake made a quick call to his wife, telling her that their six-year-old was 'fine and in expert hands.'

The line went silent before Rachel came back with a teary, 'Thank Christ.' Then hung up, probably no longer able to speak with a rush of that same relief that had overtaken Jake.

Jake and Charlotte went back through the myriad of hallways to the busy main waiting room. Jake told his daughter to take a seat while he went outside to pay the taxi driver. He felt very indebted to the driver and felt bad about abandoning him in the hospital car park. Jake hoped he would understand because—

He slowed to a standstill as he crossed the accident and emergency car park. The city taxi was parked in the same awkward spot where the driver had left them, at an angle in the ambulance bay. Ambulance drivers had gathered around the car, complaining that

148

it was in the ambulance parking area. The back door was still open, but there was no sign of the driver. The taxi's engine was idling, and the headlights were on full blast. Thinking he missed something, Jake spoke to the ambulance drivers and asked where the driver had gone. They shook their heads in puzzlcment. They were just as curious as Jake because the car was illegally parked. The vehicle was not causing any obstruction to the ambulances, but the taxi driver should have known that it wasn't permitted. 'He would've driven into the waiting room if the car fit through the doors,' commented another member of the ambulance team.

Jake went back inside to the information desk where he met the friendly lady he had first met in his panic. Through the hatch in the glass wall, he said, 'Sorry to bother you, but do you have any idea where the driver of the taxi out there in the ambulance bay has got to? He brought us here, and I never paid him. We just left him stranded.' Jake went on to tell her about their unwonted adventure. 'I feel bad about it now. If it wasn't for his, um, driving skills…'

'*Crazy* driving skills,' Charlotte interjected. '*Crazy good* driving skills.'

'…my daughter wouldn't be alive right now.' Jake Montgomery finished as he broke down as the night's fluttering nerves, sweat, and stress caught up with him for a second time. Charlotte had never seen her father cry before and it was something else she would take with her from this strange night that started so

149

sweetly with her little sister's sixth birthday and the joke candles.

The woman craned her neck to get a view of the taxi. She considered him for a moment before turning to her colleagues. Their words went unheard behind the thick wall of glass. She came back to them. 'Y'know,' she said to Jake and Charlotte with a curious smile, 'that's the fourth time this week that has happened. A different taxi every time.'

Jake and Charlotte exchanged glances.

She went on to tell the Montgomerys that the other taxis pulled right up into the ambulance docking area, which was the closest point to the main doors of the A&E department. 'All very strange.' She shook her head.

A week later, when Eva's nut reaction was but a bad memory, Jack Montgomery opened his MacBook to read the city news. His eyes fixated on an article with a simple yet catchy title:

Ghost Taxi Driver

Over the last number of weeks, staff at Limerick City Hospital have been witnessing strange occurrences during the twilit hours in the city. It began three weeks ago when a young child arrived at the A&E with his mother. The girl had drunk bleach and was gravely ill. The mother who doesn't have a car called 112. An ambulance was sent to their address on the city outskirts. When a taxi pulled up at the front door, the mother didn't question why a taxi was there with the back door open instead of an ambulance, waiting for them to jump inside. According to the mother of the child, the driver said next to nothing except, "I'm the best taxi driver in the city," which he repeated over and over.

And this is where Jake's eyes did a double take. He re-read that line again. "I'm the best taxi driver in the city."

The taxi was abandoned on the hospital premises. It was later discovered that the vehicle was stolen from a taxi driver earlier the same evening while he was helping tourists to a hotel with their luggage. A similar event occurred the following night when two parents brought in their daughter, who had her leg bitten by the neighbour's dog. She had lost a lot of blood. The child will live to tell the tale because of the fast action of a mystery taxi driver. This reporter contacted the parents of the girl who want to express gratitude publicly to the mystery taxi driver. "Whoever you are out there, we hope you see this. You saved our little girl. Thank you from the bottom of our hearts."
Again, the driver declared to them he was "…the best taxi driver in the city" as they sped through the city. The police later retrieved the discarded taxi and returned it to its rightful owner.

Jake Montgomery forgot to breathe as he read through the last paragraph. His skin broke out in goosebumps and the hairs on the nape of his neck and arms stood on end.

There is mounting speculation that the mystery taxi driver is the spirit of a local taxi driver who was involved in a fatal car accident with his passengers earlier this year when he lost control of his vehicle and collided with a goods truck on Henry Street while on his way to Limerick City Hospital's Accident & Emergency department with two passengers who also lost their lives in the head-on collision. The grieving mother told this newspaper her husband was taking their daughter to the A&E because she had shoved not one but two crayons up her nose and was finding it difficult to breathe. Perhaps the taxi driver never left Henry Street, where he and his passengers lost their lives. Maybe he is trying to make up for mistakes in death that he made in life. Who knows?

Remembering to breathe again, Jake closed his MacBook. He got up from the table, walked over to the living room window and looked out across the city skyline, wondering who, where, and what had driven them to the hospital that night and saved his daughter's life. And his own.

Dead End

Dead-Ends 8

Crossbreed

When the Mackenzie family set off on their yearly camping trip, they didn't know they would and wouldn't be returning home.

There was great excitement that mid-July morning when the four Mackenzies and Scruff, the family mutt, piled into the shoddy old camper van for their yearly camping trip in the wilds of Old Castle's National Park, which was a four-hour drive away, down in the south-west of the country. 12-year-old Jason and his 14-year-old sister Layla sat in the back with Scruff while their mom and dad, Brendan and Elizabeth, were up at the front. Elizabeth was driving while Brendan played his own songs on his guitar. Let's just say his family was a captive audience. Despite Bob-Dylan-wannabe Brendan's erratic performance, life was good.

But like everything else on the weighing scales of life, the Mackenzies would have to take the good with the bad.

Sixteen long Brendan songs later, the Mackenzie's camper van pulled into a café on a secluded stretch of road. Jason was feeling nauseous in the back seat with all the sharp turns on the snaking road, and his father's music didn't help. Jason had never been a good traveller. As a child, he would feel sick on the short ride to school — especially on days he didn't feel like going to school. And now the 12-year-old was queasy with his father's lacklustre songs, not that he would say that to his dad. On the sly, his mother and sister thanked him for his impromptu bout of nausea.

They went inside the café, where the clientele comprised of hikers and families, just like the Mackenzies. Even though the owners of the café were a pleasant young couple, they weren't too fond of the idea of allowing the little tearaway terrier into their eating establishment, so the Mackenzies obliged and kept Scruff in the camper van, leaving the windows cracked. He preferred his old basket, anyway.

They were halfway through a round of ham and pickle rolls when the four Mackenzies paused and shared ominous glances around the table before breaking down in peals of laughter. The midday local news channel was coming from a portable TV at the end of the counter, and the newsreader announced that a family of four, not too different from the Mackenzies, had gone missing in the area a few days previous and if anyone had any information on the family's whereabouts, they were to call a number that came up on the screen. According to the newsreader, they vanished off the radar after a camping trip in the remote area of Abbeyleith. She told the studio camera that several people had gone missing in that general area over the last two weeks.

Despite the worrying news report, the family couldn't help their reaction of hilarity, just biting into their tasty rolls when they all paused, mouths open. It was a nervous gut-buster of laughter because the family in the photo on the screen didn't look all that different from them. It was this resemblance that sent a tenebrous flutter through the Mackenzie clan.

This would be their last genuine feel-good moment, despite what was on the little telly. It was lamentable that they didn't appreciate it. But does anyone appreciate the good times? They may think they do until they are in the bad times and look back on the good times and realise they never appreciated what they had.

Elizabeth said to her husband. 'I saw that Abbeyleith on the map. It's near to here.'

The Mackenzies were on a roll now and this comment was met with more laughs.

Once Jason was feeling better, they all got back in the camper van and headed west towards the national park. The news report was but a fading memory.

Brendan, whose turn it was to drive, tapped on his Google Maps icon on his phone to check for directions when Elizabeth told him to, 'Put it away, for the love of God. All these *helpful* apps,' flashing air commas on *helpful*, 'are turning us braindead. Haven't you ever noticed how you have no idea how you arrived at a destination if you used Google Maps to get there? We are being spoon-fed: *At the next roundabout, take the third exit on the right,* as if we were mentally slow…and that's where we're going, by the way. When I was young, we used road signs and a map. And we remembered how we got to a place because we had to figure it out. We don't need GPS, Brendan. Look out there in front of you. Rant over.'

The twin peaks of Mag Reek mountain rising high in the hazy distance marked their destination.

'We agreed we wouldn't use our phones on this trip. "Getting back to nature." Your words, Brends, not mine.'

'You're right! Bad habit, that's all.' Brendan Mackenzie switched off his phone and left it in the glove compartment. 'These phones are shrinking our brains.' He pulled his finest twisted zombie face for his wife and laughed.

'You hear that, kids?' Elizabeth asked.

'Hmm?' Layla replied, watching Netflix on her phone.

Jason looked up from his tablet with a lost expression. 'Have we arrived?'

'Guys,' Brendan said in the rearview mirror as he put the camper van into gear and drove away from the café car park, 'you're missing out on life.'

'No, we're not,' said Layla. 'We're as alive sitting here in the back of the van as anywhere else.'

'But don't you want to see this beautiful countryside? Right now, you could be at home in your bedroom. When you're looking at a screen, it doesn't matter where you are. You're trapped.'

'Dad,' said Jason, 'I'm not trapped. I'm playing Roblox with Robert and Liam.'

Brendan shook his head. 'This is pointless. The sense of adventure and getting lost doesn't exist with these fucking devices. Whatever happened to the expression live a little? I wish they never invented these things, especially phones.'

'Well,' opined Elizabeth, 'you have to change your way of thinking. Phones are here to stay, I'm afraid. And you cannot deny how useful they are when you want to know where the kids are.'

How poignant Elizabeth's words would be on this very day.

'Hey,' said Brendan, 'I thought you were on my side?'

'I am. All I'm saying is that we need to be realistic but put firm limits. I mean, do we really need to be lost?'

'Liz, I'm not talking about lost as literally lost. I'm talking about the camping trip into the wilds, losing the shackles. Having that sense of freedom. Our kids don't know what that is anymore. Sometimes, it's good to get lost.'

'I wish you'd get lost, Dad,' said Layla without missing a beat or looking up from her screen.

Brendan laughed, as did his wife. They shouldn't, but their daughter's sense of dry wit and timing was wicked.

But Brendan sobered up when he saw the looming thunderheads in the distance.

Not twenty minutes up the road from the café, Elizabeth Mackenzie was taking back her words about not needing Google Maps. Brendan and his wife exchanged tentative glances, both experiencing that sinking feeling as if they had just driven through an invisible barrier into the unknown. Their gut instincts told them they were lost. They were lost since the moment they left the café, about the same time Brendan switched off his phone, ironically enough. Brendan remembered taking a left off the main road when he probably shouldn't have. Somewhere along the way, they made a wrong turning and were now on a back road that didn't see many vehicles. None, in fact. They just knew if they mentioned the *lost* word, then the kids would be the first to berate them with something like—

'Are we lost?' asked Jason.

The kids may have been living in an alternative reality as far as Brendan and Elizabeth were concerned, but all Jason had to do was take one look out the window and he knew they were lost.

'Jason, sometimes it's good to get lost,' quipped Layla. 'Didn't you know that?'

The thunderstorm had crept its way in from the Atlantic and was now over the Mackenzies' camper van. The camper filled with white noise as the rain bucketed down.

Brendan turned to his wife. 'Now is it safe to check Google Maps?' He eased his foot off the accelerator.

'You're hilarious,' droned Elizabeth.

'Because I don't see Mag Reek anymore, Liz.'

Elizabeth scanned the area. It was true. The rain was so heavy they couldn't see much further than the thickets on their left and right. 'Okay, so we're useless without our phones. It's official. Let's just love our phones.'

Jason said, 'Scruff needs the toilet.'

The family dog had got up from his basket and was sniffing around the back door.

'Me too,' chimed Layla.

'And me,' added Jason.

'Guys, it's lashing out there. You could've gone when we were back at the café.'

'But I didn't need to go then, Dad,' said Layla. Her brother nodded in agreement.

'Brendan, don't be silly. That involves foresight.'

Brendan sighed. 'This is just typical.' He asked the dog, 'Scruff? You need to go pee?'

The dog gave a wheezy half-hearted yap, which wasn't really a bark. The dog hadn't barked for years.

'That's a number two bark, Dad.'

'Scruff doesn't bark,' Layla said.

'You get what I mean,' Jason back-answered. 'We need to let him out, Dad.'

Elizabeth added, 'I think I need to go, too. Just pull over here somewhere. It'll give us a chance to get our bearings too.'

Brendan pulled the camper van up on the secluded stretch of road, deciding he needed the bathroom as well. 'If you can't beat 'em, join 'em!'

They coated up, jumped out, and went their separate ways into the undergrowth for a little privacy. Scruff wasn't too bothered about privacy.

When Brendan was zipping up, he spotted a lone grey farmhouse down in the vale, surrounded by a

159

thick copse of conifer trees. The kind found in cemeteries. 'Hey, there's a house over there!' He announced to the others.

'What about it?' Layla called back, out of sight and squatting amongst some dock leaves. 'It's not as if we're *lost*.'

'We're in the middle of fucking nowhere,' Jason called from the bushes.'I read somewhere that the weirdest shit happens in places like this.'

This back-and-forth was like the last scene from *The Waltons*, where the Walton family says goodnight to each other from different bedrooms.

Elizabeth replied, 'Thanks for that, Jason,' from the undergrowth.

'You're welcome,' her son replied. 'Hey, wouldn't it be hilarious if someone—' robbed the camper van and drove off while we're out here pissing up against trees...were the very words that dried up in the 12-year-old's throat when they all heard the camper van rev up...

The Mackenzies came from the vegetation, struggling to pull up zips and latch buttons.

'What the f...' was all Elizabeth had time to say as she jumped out of the ferns, struggling to pull her jeans up.

The four Mackenzies stood there in dumb shock, literally caught with their trousers down as the camper van barrelled by them, fishtailing down the wet secondary road, its shocks rattling in the rain-filled potholes. It was almost as if the old camper had started up on its own and drove off without them.

Like an old friend had just turned traitor on them. Battered it may be, but that camper van had been with the Mackenzie family since the beginning and the kids would grow up remembering the old camper van.

'Someone just stole our van!' Layla screamed, pointing out the obvious.

Brendan cried, 'Did anyone see or hear anything?'

Nobody had seen or heard anything.

Brendan reached for his phone to call the police and swore to the high heavens when he realised he'd left his phone on the dashboard. 'Who else has their phones?!' He looked around at the others in desperation. 'We need a phone! Elizabeth, call the police!'

'My fucking phone's in the van!'

Layla flashed that look at her.

'Don't start!' snapped her mother. 'We don't need whatever smart-ass answer you're about to give us now.'

'I said nothing,' Layla retorted. 'But it's just that Dad was going on about ditching our phones and getting lost, and well...'

'Layla!' came her mother's whiplash tongue. 'Shut it!'

'Fuck!' Brendan swore. 'Now, what are we going to do?'

'Maybe we can go down to that house and ask them for help,' suggested Jason. 'The one you said you saw, Dad. Where did you say that the house was?'

His mother nodded. 'Okay, Jason. Good! See,

Layla? This is what we need right now — positive input.'

But Layla wasn't listening. The 14-year-old was looking around her in confusion.

Brendan led his family to the point in the tree line where he saw the house. It was quite far away, tucked down inside a wooded valley.

Layla cried. 'Scruff!'

The others turned around, expecting to see the dog behind them, but there was no sign of the happy little canine.

'Where is he?' asked Elizabeth.

'Oh shit,' said Jason. 'I think I saw him climb back into the camper. He loves his basket.'

Layla started to cry. Seeing Layla's reaction set off a panic alarm in Elizabeth. Brendan, too, felt the first flutter of fear but tried to keep it hidden. 'Don't worry. We're going to go across there and get help. Whoever stole the van might not even notice Scruff in his basket.'

Layla asked, 'But what if they do?'

'Layla, Scruff is fine. They stole the van, they didn't steal Scruff. They weren't looking to steal a van with a dog in it.'

'Mom, Scruff won't even notice it's not us driving the van. He won't bark. He's too old to bark!'

'And maybe it's better that way,' answered Elizabeth. 'We don't want him to aggravate whoever is behind the wheel of our camper van.' She turned to her husband. 'So, what now?'

'We're going down to that house,' Brendan pointed

out.

Elizabeth eyed the lone farmhouse. 'I think we should turn back the way we came. I don't like the look of that place.'

Brendan pointed out, 'In case you hadn't noticed, we are sort of in a crisis here. No phones.'

Layla was about to pipe up when her father face-palmed her. 'Liz, whether you like the look of the place is not important right now. I need to get our van and we need to get our stuff. We have everything in the van.'

Layla interjected, 'Nobody cares about Scruff!'

'Layla,' said Brendan, 'we all love Scruff, but right now, we have more important matters at hand. 'Our phones are not the only things tied up in the camper van—our wallets, purses, and everything else.'

Elizabeth was growing more distressed. 'Our identity cards were in that van!'

'2023 has been the worst year for identity theft,' Jason pointed out. He wouldn't have known this, only he was interested in cyber security and hackers fascinated him.

The Mackenzies would be the victims of identity theft, but not in the way they thought it would happen.

'We need to get out of here and find someone who can help us. Do you understand?'

Layla shook her head in tough defiance. She didn't want to listen to her father. He wasn't as close to Scruff as she was. Which was more important — a stupid phone or Scruff? C'mon, that was no competition.

The Mackenzie family set off down the country lane — the same lane their camper van had used in the getaway. It lashed rain and moody thunder rumbled above their heads. As they marched to the sounds of their squelching boots, Brendan wondered what they would find at the end of this little travelled by-road.

As the Mackenzies drew nearer the property, they walked right by a road sign overgrown and hidden beneath a clump of brambles, telling them they were now in the nowhere district of Abbeyleith.

*

Five minutes up the winding road with a strip of green grass snaking through its middle, four individuals were moving along a country road in a rickety camper van, travelling at insane motorway speeds on a country by-road. The van shunted left and right. It might or might not have been the driver's first time at the wheel of a vehicle. It might or might not have been the driver's first time seeing a dashboard and wondering what those pretty coloured lights meant. A little terrier cowered in its basket in the interior of the camper van. The dog may be old, but the clever little terrier sensed something wasn't right. The scent rising in his glistening snout told him the four occupants of the vehicle were not his loved ones. These four individuals didn't sound like his loved ones — they didn't sound like his clan because they didn't make any noise like the others. There was silence in the bouncing, shuddering camper van. Yet the canine was confused. Maths wasn't the terrier's strong point, but it sensed the number in his clan — four — was correct. At least, from its beady eyes, the dog distinguished four human figures. But again, the old dog sensed there was something off just by their stillness. His normal clan made incessant noise and moved about the place. These four — two in the back and two in the front — may as well be statues. Throughout its thirteen years on this planet, the aged dog had encountered many humans, but never had it experienced a scent like what it was encountering in its olfactory system now. A miasma replaced the familiar clan smell, and it made the terrier's hindquarters tremble. The dog cowered in its shabby basket. It never much discerned its clan's eyes, could never make them out in the general head area, instead going by scent and sound, but the dog sensed those lifeless stares now.

For the first time in years, the bow-legged terrier barked.

*

The farmhouse was further away than it looked. It proved to be an optical illusion — the illusion of getting help had clouded the Mackenzie's senses. What at first was a drab farmhouse in the middle of nowhere was now a beacon of hope and had the same effect on the Mackenzies as if they were penniless, homeless and starving, and had just spotted the glowing yellow M of a McDonald's restaurant in the distance.

When the complaining kids fell back, Brendan

murmured from the corner of his mouth to his wife, 'This house has to work. You saw how far we came and we didn't see any houses. And God only knows where the next house will be.'

Elizabeth agreed. 'I'm regretting coming this way.'

'Why?'

Elizabeth cast a doubtful look at the property. 'Doesn't the house look abandoned? Even from here, I can tell that nobody lives there.'

'Liz, we're in the middle of nowhere. Look around you. That's the only house out here and we're going to make it work, no matter what happens.'

For now, Elizabeth reserved judgement.

That big old house seemed more and more vacant as they drew nearer. The half-drawn tattered lace curtains had taken on a sun-bleached ivory shade, giving the effect of dereliction and emptiness. The country house was a hollow shell.

Brendan imagined desiccated insects littering window sills in empty draughty rooms and sucked-dry bee and fly carcasses stuck in pockets of sticky cobwebs long since vacant. Not that Brendan was going to mention any of that now to his family. 'I think we're going to knock on that front door and an old farmer and his wife are going to come out to us. That's the vibe I'm getting.' That hypothetical old farming couple was the best-case scenario, and he just knew it. Brendan Mackenzie was almost positive that there was nobody at the house to invite them in, only desiccated insect shells as empty as the house they lay in. Brendan and Elizabeth linked arms and walked head first into the driving rain while the kids traipsed after them.

Ten minutes later, they were standing by the rusty buckled front gates of the house, held together by a frayed string and the Mackenzie family's fraying hope. The house was in a terrible state of disrepair. It was a two-story farmhouse with grimy pebble-dash walls and a mossy roof of black slate. They could see from the rusted gates and bountiful clumps of grass growing around the base of the mangled barrier that these gates had not been opened for a long time. The front door of the house was another fifty feet away from the gates, at the end of a narrow pathway. There wasn't any sign of a bell.

Elizabeth called out, 'Hello! Anybody home?'

No answer.

'Only the ghosts are home,' Jason surmised.

Layla hissed, 'Don't say that! You know I'm afraid of ghosts, Jay.'

'Um…yeah?' came Jason's reply.

The Mackenzies stared at the solitary house through the rain. No matter how hard they gazed at that grubby front door, it just would not open. A pervading stillness told them nobody was at home.

'I think I saw the curtain moving!' Layla said excitedly.

'That's only your imagination,' said Jason.

Brendan also thought he saw movement at the window. He considered his daughter with a keen eye. He decided there and then to call his daughter's bluff.

'Which curtain?' he asked quietly.

Layla pointed straight to the window on the right of the front door and the same window where Brendan thought he saw movement. He nodded. 'I saw the curtain move too.'

While they were looking at the front of the house, Jason wandered off. He walked a little further up the driveway and stopped dead and gawked at something in the backyard. The 12-year-old opened his mouth to speak, but no words came out. Afraid to raise suspicion, he waved frantically at his family, who were more interested in trying to figure out how to contact the owners of the house. Seeing that they didn't see or hear him, he back-pedalled to the front gate and pulled and dragged at his mother and father, puce in his panic.

Brendan turned from the house to see the frantic look on his son's face. 'Jesus, Jason!'

His mother asked, 'What's wrong?'

'Slow down, Jason,' said Layla.

The boy was hyperventilating, only able to speak in monosyllables. 'Camper van! Scruff! People!' Jason closed his eyes and marshalled every fibre of his being to control his breathing.

The 12-year-old was fearful and the others could see that fear manifest in his stark eyes, raindrops streaking down his face. Instead of speaking, Jason led the others around the side of the house, where they hid behind an overgrown elderberry bush. Brendan, Elizabeth, and Layla broke out in gooseflesh when they saw their van parked up in the backyard, away from the view of prying eyes. The shock of seeing their camper parked up behind the house was one thing, but something else was seeing four people sitting in it. They made out the silhouettes of two people in the front and two people sitting in the back. The strange thing was that they were just sitting there, like cut-outs framed in the van's interior. The Mackenzies could hear their dog's muffled barks and whines and that only added an extra layer of whipped creepy on this wedding cake for the damned.

On hearing Scruff barking, Layla slapped her hands to her mouth to stop her scream — a scream that germinated from witnessing her dog bark for the first time in a long time. It had been a few years since she'd heard Scruff bark like he was *woof-woofing* now. As age had caught up with him (after all, Scruff was 91 years old in human years), his bark deteriorated into a chesty cough.

The 14-year-old's heart ached with every distressed, piercing yap. Layla broke from the group, but Elizabeth dragged her back.

Her mother whispered, 'What are you doing? You don't know who is sitting in our van!'

'Scruff wants to get out, Mom!'

'Yes, okay, but let's think this through.'

Panicked scratching came from inside the back door of the camper van and they just knew the dog was trying to burrow his way out. It wasn't his cute paw-padding toilet call he gave now and again to let people know he needed to do his business. No, this sounded as if Scruff had been buried alive.

'Mom! What's going on?' Jason was terrified. The lad's eyes were about to pop out of his skull.

'Listen, everybody,' said Brendan, 'calm the fuck down! Vehicles are stolen every day of the week.'

Layla snapped back, 'We don't care about the stupid old van! We want Scruff!'

'And we'll get him!' hissed Elizabeth. 'But let's be clever about this!'

She turned to her husband, about to ask him what the next step was when, without warning, the camper van rumbled into life.

They pushed further in behind the sprawling elderberry bush…

Whoever was behind the wheel of the van did not know how to drive. The gears ground and cranked. Brendan winced with every tear of the cogs, just as his daughter flinched with every bark. The driver appeared to not know if he or she (though it looked like he) wanted to drive forward or reverse. The van chugged and stalled…before roaring into life and shooting backwards, screaming in high revs across the backyard and crashing into the barn. Thankfully, hay bales broke the vehicle's impact. More gear grinding ensued before the van shot forward in spurts…and spun out of the backyard, soaking them in a spray of dirty puddle water. As the van rolled by, they heard the dog's uncharacteristic howling and whining. It tugged at their heartstrings to hear the little dog cry like that. They watched the van drive away in the rain, rocket down the country lane, and then make a left, back in the same direction they'd

170

come from.

The four Mackenzies looked at each other, waiting for someone to speak.

Brendan asked nobody in specific, 'What are we going to do?'

That their father asked that question didn't give the children much hope.

Elizabeth was looking at the ground, blinking, lost in thought. 'Did you get a look at them?'

'Not really,' Brendan answered.

'I glimpsed the passenger in the front seat. She looked like a normal woman about my age. Doesn't exactly fit the car thief profile. Then again, what do I know?'

'I got a better look at the man behind the wheel,' said Jason. 'He was her husband.'

Brendan scoffed, 'How do you know that, Sherlock?'

Jason answered, 'Cos I've seen them before.'

'What are you talking about?' Brendan and Elizabeth asked in unison.

'Wait!' Layla's eyes lit up. 'I've seen them before too!'

'Layla,' started Elizabeth. 'How would you…' Her jaw dropped as the penny dropped. She, too, had seen that couple. Only their faces were different somehow. Maybe it was because of the rain, but the shiny happy family in the picture on the TV screen on the café counter weren't the same people she saw sitting in the front seat of the camper van just now. 'The news report…' she said in a trance.

Brendan raised his eyebrows and turned to the spot at the bottom of the lane where the van had disappeared. 'You mean to tell me that the people in…the…'

And Elizabeth was already nodding. 'The same people took our camper van, Brends.'

Just then, Jason's stomach growled, so loud they heard it over the whoosh of the rain. It might have been funny in other circumstances. 'I'm hungry.'

'Me too,' said Layla.

'Me three,' said Brendan apologetically. He looked at the sky. 'It's already getting dark. Let's see if we can stay here. Maybe we can find something to eat.'

'I think we should keep moving,' said Elizabeth. 'What if they come back?'

Brendan's hungry stomach fluttered with nerves. He was aware his kids were analysing everything, and he was doing his best to keep the authoritative side out, but he was struggling. 'Firstly, nobody is living in the house. Secondly, it's pouring rain and it'll be dusk before we know it.' Brendan always fell back into his Firstly and Secondly when he was under pressure and needed to get his bullet points out.

'Thirdly, I'm starving,' added Jason.

Layla was fraught with anxiety, but she agreed with her younger brother.

Elizabeth, too, was feeling the first pangs of hunger, but she held back. They didn't need any extra pressure now.

'Maybe we can get in and find something to eat. And, now that we're here, why don't we—'

'Brendan, if you think we're going to sleep in that house tonight, then you have another thing coming,' Elizabeth answered. 'I think we should keep walking down that road. I'm sure we will come out at a crossroads or something similar where we can flag someone down.' She could see everything opening out in our mind's eye; a fantasyland where a car stopped for them and her family rejoiced and hugged before climbing in. 'Then they could take us to the local police station and we can report the van missing. They will find the camper because it stands out.'

'That's one way of putting it,' quipped Jason, who was trying to keep the good side out.

'Let's take a vote on it,' suggested Brendan. 'Who votes to stay here and try to get inside the house?'

The children gazed at the brooding building through the pelting rain. It didn't look very inviting, but it was a roof over their heads. However, the creep factor emanating from the property was too much to overcome. They kept their hands by their sides, not willing to vote for their father's option.

'That's decided,' Elizabeth concluded. 'Let's go.' Without listening to any further protests, she turned and marched to the bottom of the lane and turned right, as opposed to their stolen camper van, which turned left the way they had come and where they knew there was nothing there for them. At least, not enough civilisation to bank on. The road not taken was their option for now and Robert Frost would be proud of them...

Only this wasn't the same road Frost hadn't taken,

for not ten minutes down that country lane or *botharín* as they might say down here in the wilds of the South West. They came to a dead end. The four of them stood there in the rain, looking at the point where a blackthorn hedge swallowed the road. It was an optical illusion.

'It's a dead end!' Brendan exclaimed.

'You can say that again,' replied Layla with an ominous air.

Brendan turned to his family and asked, 'So, who wants to vote for the house now?'

Reluctantly, the kids and Elizabeth raised their arms.

'We don't have to sleep inside the house. Maybe we can sleep outside it.'

Perplexed faces stared back at him. 'It will get chilly tonight, but if we all bundle in together, I'm sure we'll keep each other warm in the hay barn — it's full of hay. And we leave at first light. It gets bright at 5:30. We can be on the road and nobody will ever know we stayed there. But all of this is if we don't find anyone between now and dark.' Brendan knew the chances of that were next to none, but he kept that to himself.

Elizabeth was on the fence about it. She turned to her kids. 'Kids?'

'I think it's a good plan,' said Layla.

Jason nodded. 'Me too.'

'Maybe we don't have a choice,' Elizabeth pointed out. 'Inside or outside the house, we cannot sleep in these clothes, Brendan. They'll get pneumonia.

Maybe we can light a fire?'

Brendan smiled.

They turned and headed back towards the farmhouse, crestfallen and soaked, but with a hint of hope now.

Feeling it wasn't right to knock on the back door and give any sleeping resident in the house a heart attack, Brendan Mackenzie crept around to the front of the house and knocked. The family looked at each other, waiting for an answer, but nothing came. Brendan pushed in the rusty flap of the letter slot — a feature from a bygone era — and called inside. 'Hello? Anybody home?' He tried to sound chirpy. It was strange to imagine his voice echoing out around the house. Brendan imagined his voice echoing through the cold, damp rooms he never visited. It was a strange sensation indeed. He called again, then pressed his right ear into the slot and listened. The father of two couldn't be sure, but he thought he heard shuffling coming from somewhere at the end of the hallway. Or perhaps it was upstairs? It was difficult to tell.

Deciding the coast was clear, Brendan stole up to the back door of the house. They looked into the kitchen. It was clear then that no one had lived in this house for a few decades. It didn't matter how rough and ready the property was. Brendan knew he needed to get his cold, wet, and miserable family inside. 'Stand back,' he commanded before clinching his arm and driving his elbow through the pane of glass closest to the door handle. The sound of smashing glass filled the kitchen. Brendan angled his hand through the jagged hole. Feeling about for the key, he found the keyhole instead. 'Shit, no key.'

'And you thought the key would, I dunno, somehow just be sitting in the lock? Waiting for someone like us to smash the window and turn the key?' Layla asked.

Brendan withdrew his hand, careful not to scratch himself. While he was trying to ignore his daughter's sarcasm and considering their next move, his wife pulled down on the door handle. To everyone's surprise, especially Brendan's, the door swung in on its hinges. Elizabeth winked at Brendan and stepped into the musty kitchen. The expression on Brendan's face was laughable, and he knew for a fact that his children would have laughed in his face if they weren't so miserable. Instead, they blanked him as they walked into the interior of the farmhouse.

The place was decrepit. Nobody had lived here since the 1990s.

By now, Layla's cheeks were taking on a bluish hue, and it was her mother who noticed. 'Jesus, Layla.' Turning to her husband, Elizabeth said, 'We need to light a fire somehow.' The house was empty of furniture. 'Maybe we can find something outside in the sheds to burn. If—'

Her words dried to a gulping click when they all heard a distinct shuffling outside in the hallway, down to the right where the kitchen was. Someone or something was standing where they had just come from. They listened to the slow and deliberate crinkle and rustle of dry leaves that had migrated into the hallway. An uninvited guest tip-toed stealthily along the hallway...but weren't the Mackenzies the uninvited guests?

More feet skulking along the creaking floorboards. It was pointless trying to convince themselves that was just the old house expanding and contracting or whatever it is old houses do. No, these groaning floorboards sounded too deliberate and sickeningly obvious that they weren't alone. Brendan had tried to convince himself it was nothing more than a plump whiskered rodent, but those footfalls were too well-timed and gathered to be any fat rat. Brendan hated the furry creatures with a passion, but he would give anything to peer around the living room door now and spot a giant rat minding its own business, sniffing through the leaves. Those crunching leaves had registered with Brendan as they tip-toed through the hallway. But now the leafy debris promoted unwanted questions like how had those leaves come in? The air in here was dead in more ways than one; it didn't even have a single waft of a draft that Brendan might have felt in another dilapidated house. Those leaves had to have found their way in here somehow. His heart beat harder and a wave of fainting nausea came over him. He looked at the others with wide, petrified eyes. There was someone in the house with them. Not only that, the individual had been coming and going for quite some time judging by the buildup of tree matter around the entrance of the hallway. Then again, there was no rule against the owner of the house coming and going, yet what house owner leaves debris build up in a hallway? Many questions and not enough answers.

Brendan didn't want to scare the kids, but Jason and Layla could see fear in their father's face.

Then everything took on a sinister slant when from that shuffling in the hallway crept little feet. The Mackenzies looked at each other in dumbfounded puzzlement. Who or what was in their presence? And then came the strange grunting sounds that might have been words on a different planet. Brendan and Elizabeth shared the same shocked WTF! expression. The distance between each footfall was too short to be an adult…yet too gauged to be that of a child. But if it was a child, then what was he or she doing skulking around in this derelict building in the middle of nowhere? Worse again, what was a child doing alone in this building? But maybe even worse than any of that…what if the child wasn't alone? It was a pretty big farmhouse, and they had only seen the small section where they stood rigid right now.

Those tiny creeping footsteps inched inside Brendan Mackenzie's head. What if it wasn't a child at all, but a dwarf? A little person? A myriad of strange hallucinations filled Brendan Mackenzie's senses. But he had one thing clear: they needed to vacate this house now, and he gestured as much to the others while doing his best not to panic any of them. He was ready to panic and run like fuck out of there, and the sweat beading on his forehead gave that away.

Afraid of his life to confront whatever was right outside the living room door, Brendan considered the two windows on the far wall. They were big enough to jump through and low enough not to break a bone. He could live with a twisted ankle. Brendan tip-toed to the windows. They were old-style windows with a wooden frame that slid vertically. He went to lift the window closest to the chimney when his son hissed, 'Shh, listen!'

Everyone turned to Jason.

The 12-year-old whispered, 'I think I heard a car.'

They listened but heard nothing. The Mackenzies might've gone to one window to see if Jason had indeed heard a vehicle, but these windows were facing the front yard.

And speaking of windows…

The wooden window frame had expanded and jammed solid. Red-faced Brendan turned and called for Jason's help. Jason stepped in next to his father. The two of them took hold of the window, then heaved with all their might, but the window was stuck fast and wasn't moving. Layla and Elizabeth lent a hand but to no avail. They tried the window to the right and attempted the same. That window was just as seized up.

With a growing sense of impending doom, Brendan Mackenzie closed his eyes, took a sharp, deep breath, and exhaled. He had no choice but to confront the fifth unknown visitor to this house. The father of two stole up to the living room door and blessed himself, and that was saying something considering Brendan was a staunch atheist. Peering around the edge of the door, he saw Scruff standing there in the hallway, looking up at him. He was never so happy to see the little dog in all his life…

But something wasn't right with the terrier.

Nobody else would have noticed, but the same family who had been living with the canine for thirteen years noticed. The terrier cowered and displayed uncharacteristic behaviour. Brendan, perplexed, squatted and called the dog. 'Hey, Scr—?'

Brendan didn't have time to scream, but…

*

Just minutes before Brendan Mackenzie screamed, the Mackenzies' camper van pulled up…or rather crashed up. Four individuals stepped out of the idling van and made a deadpan beeline for the farmhouse. The thunder and rain didn't seem to bother them and the four appeared to walk with some difficulty. It might've gone unnoticed as people in their twilit years have a limp or touch of rheumatism or arthritis. But the younger man and woman who climbed out of the stolen camper behind the older man and woman shared that same awkward gait. Anyone would think they weren't in charge of their own bodies.

Behind them, a little terrier poked its nose out the back door and sniffed at the rain…sniffed at that strange smell of crossbreed wafting through the cascading raindrops. The canine turned and went back inside to its worn and warm basket which was all that was left of the little dog's dying world…

Just as the terrier did that thing that made its

owners laugh where it turned in dizzying circles to find its resting posture, they snatched the dog from the basket.

*

…but Brendan's family, standing behind him, had to scream and run, but the only option open to them was the top of the stairs at the end of the hallway. In their panic, they left the dog and their father and husband to fend for themselves. What had they seen standing there at the other end of the hallway? The Mackenzies didn't have time to process as they scrambled up the rickety stairs. Elizabeth's instincts told her to fall behind the children. She looked over her shoulder to see the family of four whom they had first seen on the TV news back at the café. The mother and father and their grown children were standing there with dead expressions; all floating in that same hypnotic bubble. But it wasn't the expressionless people that got her interest and nor was it the family that sent the children into a curdle of screaming fits. It was the creature, the daemonic creature in all its hellish glory, standing there barefoot on the carpet of dead leaves, with a smile on its face that sent shockwaves through the mother. Those shuffling feet should've been something innocent and explainable — how the mind conjures unseen horrors that only exist in the mind's disembodied, crooked eye. But this terror existed, and it went against everything Elizabeth Mackenzie had ever known or believed in. That tapping on the window of her 9-year-old bedroom wasn't a diabolical creature with long spindly black fingers but the long branches of the Elm tree. At least, that's what her doting parents told her. Mrs Mackenzie now knew her parents were lying to protect their daughter's undeveloped, fragile mind. Behind her, she heard the cracked screams coming from her husband. She'd never heard Brendan make noises like that and never wanted to hear anything like that ever again. Those were death screams; the body summoning one last S.O.S piercing alarm before lights out.

Elizabeth called out from halfway up the stairs, 'Brendan?!' But it had gone awfully quiet down there. From her angle on the stairway, she could only see a few feet of the hallway. Whatever happened, happened out of view. Maybe it was better that way. She turned to her children, but they were already gone upstairs. And for a moment, the farmhouse seemed far too quiet. Then, out of that eerie silence, came a couple of pig squeals from above her in this disturbing wave of stereo surround sound. She almost fainted when she realised those dying pigs to be gutted were her own children's cries. And just like Brendan, Elizabeth had never heard her children cry out like that…if those bloodcurdling screams had come from her children. The gruesome cries could've belonged to any teenager, male or female. But then came that deafening silence — the same silent scream that she'd heard come right after hearing her husband's last genuine cry for help.

And from this veil of darkness came the little terrier's incessant yapping, and it was this that brought Elizabeth Mackenzie to tears. Just like her family's death-throe screeches, it was the first time she'd heard their old terrier bark. What kind of stress was the canine under to rekindle his bark? His piercing alarm. Listening to their family pet was like going back in a time machine. She could almost hear her children's giggles as they played with Scruff on the back lawn. And how she would love to climb into that magic machine now as her husband appeared at the bottom of the stairs and slowly began...

But that scream! Jesus Christ in Heaven, nobody comes back from a howl like that. It makes little sense; Brendan looks — is — perfect. Not a drop of blood on him. Not a...wait...the eyes. The eyes are dead! The windows to Brendan's soul have been boarded up.

...to climb the creaking steps, peering up at her with the same unblinking, deceased eyes as the family of strangers walking behind her once-upon-a-time husband. What drove Elizabeth up the stairs to uncertain death was the vision that bloomed below when more of those dark figures with strange smiles and delirious eyes appeared behind the hypnotised — possessed? — family.

Elizabeth screamed and bounded up the stairs, running away from her husband and to her stricken children...

But a surreal horror was waiting for her at the top of the warping stairs leading up to the second floor of this nightmare. She bounded into the first bedroom she found and there, lying in a double bed, were more people with no light in their opened eyes. There were six of them lying there like sardines in a tin, staring blankly at the ceiling, arms by their sides. Sitting on their chests was one more of those impish dwarfs with a grimacing smile and lunacy in its eyes. Where they had come from and what they wanted was now beyond Elizabeth as her husband took her hand and led her to the second bedroom where—

Elizabeth shrieked, rupturing vocal cords. Seeing cataleptic Jason and Layla in the gloomy room, lying there on the bed with the other strangers. Another unearthly dark entity was sitting on Jason's chest. It had just been fiddling with his mouth for the love of Christ! She was sure of it. It turned and considered her with that stuck smile, telling Elizabeth it knew something she didn't, and she was sure she didn't want to know what that was.

She fell to her children's side and shook them awake in the bed, only they were awake, gazing through her with their dead light eyes. Whatever had happened to Brendan in that split second had also happened to her children. Brendan pulled her away. She looked into his eyes and she knew in her heart and soul that he was trying to look back into her eyes, trying to make her believe everything was okay. But he just looked through her with that lost and misty gaze, almost cross-eyed.

The lights are on, but there's nobody at home.

The creature perched on her son's chest hissed and growled at Brendan, communicating in strange tongues with Elizabeth's lost husband. In mechanical fashion, he turned from the aberration that had taken him and the others hostage and said in a voice that sounded only a little like the real Brendan's voice. 'Crossbreeds.'

Her voice quaked. 'W-What?'

'We are crossbreeds now, and we need to go home. There's work that needs to be done.' He attempted a smile, and it was painful to watch 'Those people who took our van…they're confused, that's all.' His smile faltered as he looked away in lost thought, '…to remember. I can't…'

His strange smile and words terrified Elizabeth. Tears came to her eyes. 'Oh, Brendan, what's wrong?' She sniffled through her streaming tears. 'Work? What kind of work, Brendan? What's happening?'

Brendan's eyes turned slowly to the cold thing sitting on the entity once known as Jason, then back to Elizabeth. With far-off eyes, he said, 'Shh, come lie down with me, Elizabeth.'

He says Elizabeth as if he doesn't know me…

She considered the window by the bed. If she ran fast enough, she could launch herself over the people (zombies?) and break through the pane of glass…

And fall to your death, head-first, Lizzy. She heard her mother say. Sometimes, she just needed to hear her say it.

Forgetting how she got there, she found herself lying on the bed between her sleep-awake children. Her husband looked down at her, but his gaze went down through her…the bed…and the floor. Brendan couldn't see her. Elizabeth was sure he couldn't see her, not really. But what she wasn't sure of was what

185

he could see. That was a terrifying prospect. In his altered state, Brendan wanted her to think he could see her. It was all an illusion. But what wasn't an illusion was the hideous dark face that appeared next to Brendan's. Those eyes, Jesus, those eyes weren't of or for this world. That grimace that never left its face took on a new meaning when the loathsome phantom of nightmare slowly nodded…before it came at her so fast. Elizabeth just had time to open her mouth wide to scream. That deathly screech never came because something choking got in the way of the cry the second she parted her lips. It was fast whatever it was, and it was better that way.

The Mackenzie family filed out of the farmhouse. They didn't seem to realise it was the middle of the pitch-black night. Scruff, the terrier, loyally skipped by their feet. His clan smelt strange, just like the ones he was driving around in circles with earlier. Yet, these four looked like his clan. Confused, the terrier paused and then managed to climb up the two steps into the back of the camper van. The canine found his cosy basket and twirled around in circles to find the best position. The boy and girl members of his clan always made odd, though comforting sounds (it's called laughter) when he did that. But not now. They just stared at him through eyes that weren't their own; their faces ghostly wan.

The crossbred once known as a man called Brendan only found the ignition with the tip of the key quite by accident. Everything was confusing yet strangely familiar to him as he slowly found his way around the old crock camper. He crunched the gears and drove away from the farmhouse towards their home in Dublin without his headlights on. He didn't need the headlights to see the dark road ahead. If he had switched on his headlights, they would have washed across the overgrown road sign telling them they were leaving the nowhere district of Abbeyleith.

When the Mackenzie family set off on their yearly camping trip, they didn't know they would and wouldn't be returning home.

Dead End

Dead-Ends 9

Fireman

The following story is to be developed as a full-length novel of the same title — Fireman — due for publication in late 2024

When Max Power received the alert on his pager, he expected it would be a night like any other. He was wrong.

Max was reading *Hansel and Gretel* to his daughter for the third night that week when his pager screen lit up in green. He was just getting to the section where the wicked witch wanted Gretel to climb into the oven to check if it was hot enough to bake the dough they had lovingly worked on together.

'I have to go, Dani.'

Seven-year-old Danielle, tucked into the warm crux of her father's right arm, asked, 'Aw, do you have to go now, Dad?'

'I've got to put out a fire somewhere in the city. Fires don't wait for anyone, you know that.'

'But why doesn't somebody else do it?'

Max rolled his eyes. 'Because I'm a firefighter on-call,' wiggling his pager in his fingers. 'While on-call, I am waiting for a call. I already explained this to you. Remember?'

Although Danielle was aware of the answer, she chose not to respond.

'There's someone out there in the city tonight who needs my help. Maybe it's a little girl just like you.'

While I'm reading Hansel and Gretel to you, Dani, that little girl is screaming for help. She really is in the witch's oven. You won't find that in your fairy tales.

This is what Max Power wanted to tell his daughter, but she was too young to understand. Maybe it was the mean-spirited Max lurking inside him. Others would argue it was the honest Max whispering to his conscience. The firefighter had seen too much in his two decades to take this lightly. It had impaired his world vision. Being a doting father, Max shielded his little princess from the cruel realities. But a part of him wanted her to know what would happen to Gretel if she found herself in the witch's baking oven with no way out. He wanted Danielle to know why he left the house so often at strange hours and when they were in the middle of doing something together, like tonight.

'So, permission to leave, Major Danielle Power?'

The seven-year-old nodded with a sulking pout. 'I guess so.'

'Don't worry, I'll read the rest of the story to you tomorrow night. Since I've already read Hansel and Gretel to you, um, twice already this week, I'm pretty sure you know how it ends.'

They shared a knowing smile. But even though his seven-year-old daughter knew how the fairytale ended, Max wouldn't get that opportunity to read her the rest of *Hansel and Gretel*, and that was something he would take to his grave.

'Daddy?'

Max stopped at Danielle's door and turned. 'Yeah?'

'If you see another girl like me in a burning house, please save her and give her a big hug for me. Tell her that everything is going to be just fine.'

Max smiled, but his daughter's unusual request gave him pause for thought. 'Dani, I'll be here when you wake in the morning.'

And this was another line the firefighter would recall over the coming hours, days, and weeks. Seemingly thoughtless lines would play over and over in his head, on a loop.

'Maybe it's just a cat stuck in a tree, Daddy?'

Max went to his daughter's bed, hugged her, and tucked Danielle in. 'Maybe.' He kissed her on the forehead.

Downstairs, Max popped his head into the living room. 'Vee, I just got the dreaded call.' Max grimaced for comic effect. It was more for his benefit than his wife's.

Virginia turned from the TV screen. 'Oh?'

'Yep. Fire over in North Strand.'

'Oh, North Strand?' She repeated with a face of disdain. They both knew what that yucky face implied. 'Please be careful.'

He chuckled to himself. 'I'm always careful, Virginia. The ones who play with fire are the ones who need to be careful.'

'No, I mean The Strand. I'm more afraid of that

place than a fire.'

Locals referred to North Strand as The Strand. And everybody in the city knew it was nowhere near the beach. Not even the sun shone in The Strand. At least, that's how it seemed to those living outside the hellhole neighbourhood. It was true for Virginia. Even the postman didn't venture there. Every second house was boarded up or burnt to the ground and crooks lived in the houses still standing. Those houses that were still standing were at the mercy of arsonists looking for a quick insurance payout, and Max was already of the opinion that this fire he was on his way to was an insurance job.

'They don't know how to make a decent living up there, Vee. Sometimes I want to let the rats burn.'

'Now, now,' Virginia quipped. 'Be a professional, Max.'

'Whatever,' he chimed. 'Don't wait up. See you in the morning.'

Virginia was already engrossed in her latest Netflix show, forgetting her conversation with her husband. 'Hmm?'

'I said Netflix is killing books and stealing our brains.'

Virginia half turned to her husband, but her gaze remained fixed on the screen. 'Hmm? What's that, dear?'

Max sniggered and closed the door behind him.

It was such a silly throwaway moment, one of thousands in their lives. Not for a second did Max Power think this scene was to be the last scene of this theatre play he had acted out with his wife. Its sheer silliness and normality would play over in his head, just like his 'goodbye' with Danielle. This pointless banter would be their last conversation, and in time, Max Power would question the absurdity of life. If only he could've gone back in time and made it a little more special, like a peck on the lips, something to mark the moment. Instead, Virginia was stuck to the TV, watching some actors spouting lines while her husband complained about Netflix and how it was shrinking our brains. In reality, Max loved Netflix just as much as his wife did. Such a pointless finale. Perhaps it was the best way, as Max Power would not have ventured outside his door if he knew what awaited them.

Max Power parked up in the fire station car park. He jogged to the changing room, where he geared up in his heat-resistant Kevlar suit and was on the truck with his team within two minutes. The firefighters moved in silence, every man and woman knowing the drill…only this was no drill. This was the real thing, and Max Power never forgot his first night on the job when he pulled charred kids from a burning Nissan Micra. The trio of teenagers were on their way to a disco when speed ended their young lives. The teenagers were going nowhere fast and never even realised it when one of a hundred electricity pylons along the motorway cut the little Japanese import in two perfect halves, right down the middle, like a worker slicing through hotdog buns at a busy hot dog stand.

Max reached into his pocket for his earbuds. But it wasn't the reason he went sifting around. He found a coin. 'Heads or tails?'

The other four called, 'Heads!' and 'Tails!'

One by one, the five were whittled down to one: Max. Go figure.

Max plugged in his earbuds and listened to Tom Rosenthal's 'Lights Are On' to cool his nerves. The firefighter always listened to this soothing tune as they screamed their way through the night city towards a blazing inferno where melting heat, the crash of metal and rubble, and hair-raising screams awaited him with loving, open arms. They raced through the streets, with blue and red lights flashing and the siren wailing through the night. As they rocketed through the city streets, traffic pulled out of their way for these unsung heroes of dusk.

As they drew nearer to North Strand, the firefighters caught sight of the orange bloom on the skyline and the ghostly plumes billowing into the still night sky.

Max looked out his window to the left and spotted the forsaken houses rushing by, abandoned and burnt out, just empty shells where only memories of happier days lingered in the air. It made him appreciate what he had achieved in life and he was never more looking forward to going for a walk in the park on the other side of the city, with Danielle, maybe feeding the ducks in the pond. Those ducks never failed to bring his daughter to giggling fits.

Those giggles worked like a catching virus on her father and he, too, giggled with the *quack-quack* tail-twiddling ducks.

As the fire truck pulled up on the street, the five individuals sitting in that truck watched the trail-blazing flames curl and lick from the four windows of the terraced house, like a demonic skull and fiery tongues. Yep, this was arson-for-hire — insurance fraud. Max was almost fully sure of it. It was not unusual for individuals to set fires in The Strand intending to collect insurance money.

But what they were about to find inside that raging inferno caused Max Power to question his assumption…and his very existence in more ways than one.

A huddled group of on-looking neighbours stood by on the opposite side of the street, ranting about how their adjoining houses could catch fire. The burning house was one of fifteen properties in one continuous row. The rough-and-ready neighbours also hissed and spat about the occupants of the unassuming house, crying out about all kinds of people going into that place day and night. One of the group came to Max in confidence and told him it was '…a drug house'. The same individual who told him this information didn't have a single tooth in his head, and he considered Max with sunken, haunted hollows for eyes. Max didn't doubt the young man wasting away before him as he unrolled the hose had probably been a customer in that very house.

Max ordered everyone to stand back. The

firefighters sprung into action, each man and woman of the five-person team working in perfect synchronisation. Max had lost the coin toss (or won the coin toss, depending on the day and the firefighter), so it was to be himself to lead the way into the house and search for occupants, dead or alive. Max checked himself quickly and knocked on his face mask and helmet to make sure they were solid and ready. For the third time, he took three deep gulps through his SCBA (self-contained breathing apparatus), then entered the inferno.

He had a pretty good idea the house was empty. The owners would've made sure they happened not to be at the property when the place just happened to go up in flames. He battled through the raging firestorm. Nobody ever thought about the roar of a fire unless they happened to be a firefighter. Few considered the roaring bellows of an out-of-control fire, fixated only on the heat and destruction. And this one screamed inside his helmet as he made his way through the front door and down the hallway. Every room was on fire. The first room on the right was what he took to be the living room, judging by the flaming armchairs and sofa. Max did a quick reconnaissance of the room and left it behind. It was empty. Across the hallway, he entered what could only be the kitchen, making out melting appliances like the fridge and washing machine. Taking a deep breath, he appeared through the flames and smoke at the stairs. The bannister was on fire and was chewing into the steps It was now or never. Max made his way up the steep stairway to the second floor where he first found a toilet that had escaped the fire, but the raging flames unfurling from the room across the way told him this was where the fire had started, judging by the walls and his experience. He felt his way through the smoke, breathing through his SCBA…

Max Power stalled in the hallway. Through the doorway of the second bedroom, the firefighter laid eyes on something through the swirling plumes of choking fumes.

You know it's no illusion. You've smelt burning flesh before, Maximilian. The sweet aroma is a sour stomach-turner and those rich overtones of tanning leather are seeping into your face mask.

At first, the firefighter thought it was an optical illusion in which the smoke and licking flames created images, like looking up at the clouds and finding elephants and tigers in them. However, these were no exotic animals, but two human beings, each twitching mass of flesh shackled with chains onto the bottom legs of the burning double bed.

'Jesus!' Max screamed through his mask as he fell towards the two burning figures.

Suddenly, this routine house fire had turned into something much darker.

Heart thumping now, Max stepped into the inferno.

The man chained to the far end of the bed sat on the ground, head slumped forward, and too still in the flames as the fire chewed and sizzled his muscle and tissue. He was gone. Anybody could see that. When

—

But Max spasmed around to the other individual — a second man whose skin was already tearing away in the heat...when he watched his head swivel towards the doorway. The firefighter thought it was the dying body's reaction to the 600-degree Celsius flames as the nerves succumbed to the heat, tendons tightening and shrivelling, his burning neck muscles contracting and causing his joints to flex, giving the macabre impression of life in death. He reminded Max Power of a mannequin found in the medical university. The fire had already eaten through a lot of his epidermis and was working into the lower layers of subcutaneous tissue. Max assumed the man was already dead; carbon monoxide poisoning made sure he was no more. He stared at the burning individual through the crackling firestorm as his head turned to face the doorway in one last posthumous—

What came next happened in a flurry of confusion...

Bristling, dread-filled fear skittered through Max Power. Inside his Kevlar outfit, the hairs on his neck and arms prickled. He followed the dead man's line of vision, and even before Max turned to the hallway, he could see something to his left through his face mask. There, framed in the fiery doorway, Max Power laid eyes on a man silhouetted in the flames. Jesus Christ in heaven, but he could not put this down to imaginary elephants and tigers. How could he? The burning man — Fireman — stared at him and the two deceased individuals chained to the disintegrating bed. How was this even possible as the flames hissed, licked, and roared about him? But wait… He was on fire for the love of Christ?! Max Power had seen a lot down through the years, but that would be a first. He had never seen such a strange case, but he had read and heard about individuals on fire who didn't even know they were going up in flames because adrenaline was in the driving seat, like headless chickens running blind about the place.

For the first time in his career, Max Power fought the urge to run screaming from that room as his eyes crept back to the occupant sitting next to him, manacled to the double bed which was only a useless and tragic pile of melting plastic and smoking cinders. Was it just a coincidence that his head spun in the doorway's direction at that moment as the lethal effects of the heat cooked him alive? Or was he trying to tell Max something about the fireman as death took him far away? He was overcome with a throbbing pang of pity for the hostage on the floor next to him — hostage? Yes, there was no other way to look at it. He would never truly know the answer, but whatever way he looked at it, that man who had died right before his eyes had alerted him to the third individual in the burning house…and only now was it beginning to sink in that Max was standing in a murder scene. Intentional or not, Max wasn't privy to that answer for now. Had these two individuals been burnt to death or had something gone wrong?

These two individuals were goners. Now the firefighter's responsibility was to salvage what he could from this wreck. There was still a living man on the property. Whether this individual was involved in this fire and the deaths of these men was still unknown. On a professional level, it didn't matter one damn; Max Power had to save the sinners. He was a sucker for punishment.

In his blinkered vision, he rushed to get through the doorway but stumbled over burning debris and went down hard. In that brief hiatus between hitting the floor and locking his eyes back on Fireman…only there was no Fireman. He had scampered, leaving Max's blood chilled. He had something to do with this. Only a guilty man would run like—

But he was on fire! Any man is going to run when he's on fire, dammit! He might not be running in the right direction, but he'll run, by God!

At that same nanosecond, Max couldn't help but wonder whether the dead man he was lying next to had made one final desperate attempt to tell him who was responsible for this carnage before he slipped away. Perhaps that was a leap of faith. Yet, many scenarios could have led to the house fire. Maybe Max had stumbled in on a strange sex game gone wrong? If that was the case, it was something he would never understand and wouldn't want to if he could. Chains? Bedroom? Three men? Hello?

He got to his feet, not as fast as he would have liked with the heavy Kevlar suit and steel toe-capped leather boots. The firefighter stumbled out into the hallway just in time to see the third man disappear down the disintegrating stairs in a blazing trail at a velocity that turned Max's stomach. The man moved with the lethal ease of a flame.

'Phil!' Max screamed down the stairs. 'Stop him! Stop him!'

His teammate was already coming up the stairs when Max heard Phil cry back, 'Who, Max?'

He called back in a clipped tone. 'Down the stairs! Tripped! Didn't have time to catch him! Two deceased…bed…chains!'

Phil got to the top of the smouldering steps. They both stood on the landing, engulfed in smoke.

'But he…' started Max. 'I saw him go down…'

'Nobody came by me, Max.'

Max Power bellowed through his face mask. 'I just saw him jump down the fucking stairs! You had to have seen him, Philly!' Max watched his friend and fire-busting crew member shake his head adamantly. 'But…' Max felt nauseous as a fainting, clammy wave washed over him. He knew Phil and had no reason to doubt him. They had shared some hair-raising moments and Phil always kept a level head. And that level head was still replying in the negative. Max scratched his head through his Kevlar hood, flummoxed and out of his depth. He gestured over his shoulder. Phil took that as his cue to go inside the bedroom. He returned seconds later and informed Max he would fetch the body bags.

'No,' said Max. 'This is a crime scene, Philly. Nothing can be touched. Call the police. They can apply for a search warrant. Let's put out the fire with as little damage as possible.'

An hour later, the house in The Strand was nothing but a sad and wet pile of soggy black, steaming memories. The fire investigators were already up there on the second floor, cordoning off the gruesome scene. They had already asked the crew about what they had seen and heard. Max was the only member of the fire crew to have seen a third man whom nobody else could account for. But somewhere in that mountain of charred debris lay the tangible memory of 'Fireman' as Max Power would come to know him in his nightmares. And he would come to him in his nightmares…

It rises from the funeral pyre of rubble, ash and scorched memories to stare Max in the eyeballs, stand right over him in his lonely bed and whisper a hissing, fire-branding warning in his dreams, 'Ashes to Ashes, Dust to Dust…' repeatedly, so close to his face he can feel the heat emanating from the fiery lick of its crispy tongue. Fireman is trying to tell him something he already knows, but Max doesn't know it yet. Wake up, damn you! It's staring you in the face…

When the fire crew were clearing up to go home, one neighbour, an elderly woman, approached Max and told him that the two deceased individuals were professional burglars and 'didn't have a good bone to rub between them.' She also added, 'God forgive me, but the world is a better place without them tonight.' Her ominous words gave Max the chills. He pondered how she would even know two men had died in the fire — that was confidential for now. But the grapevine's tendrils had a long reach in places like

The Strand. Max took this opportunity to ask the woman if she'd ever seen a third man living in the house. She looked about her with a spooked expression on her wrinkled face. 'That place was busier than a hooker's takeaway.'

When it came to a hooker and a takeaway, Max understood the individual terms, but was unsure of their combined meaning. 'So, does that mean…?'

'People were coming and going from the place at all hours of the day and night. Lots of bad connections in that house.' She wriggled her gnarled fingers.

'Uh-huh.' The fact that it was a drug house…or a hooker's takeaway, didn't help. If so many people were in and out of that place, then that made forensics a nightmare.

'How did the fire start?' she asked.

'We don't know,' Max answered, which was the truth, but he kept the mysterious circumstances of the fire to himself for now. As he wound up the last hose, he asked her, 'Did you see anyone around the house during the fire?'

She stalled, not understanding his question. She gestured to the sizeable crowd that had gathered by now.

No, I mean a man on fire running from the building... Max smiled. 'Fair comment.' Perplexed, he thanked the woman and finished up what he was doing. He dropped one of the fire blankets as he piled them into the back of the truck. As Max reached down to grab the blanket, something caught his eye underneath the fire truck. He got down on his two knees to see a manhole cover. That was an accident waiting to happen. But as he got to his feet, Max stalled. 'Phil?'

Phil was busying himself around the fire truck. 'Yeah?'

'You drove tonight, right?'

'You know I drove tonight, Max. I drive every night.'

'C'mere.' He called Phil over and told him to have a look beneath the truck. 'Did you see that when you were parking up?'

Phil was on his hands and knees, gazing beneath the belly of the fire truck. 'See what?'

'It's easy to see, Phil. The manhole cover…'

'Yeah, I see it.'

Phil's nonplussed reaction confused Max. 'Well, did you see it when you parked up? You had to have seen the cover lying on the street with an open sewer, ready for someone to fall into it.'

Phil pulled himself to his feet and considered his friend. 'What's got into you tonight?'

'I don't follow.'

He said nothing but gestured under the fire truck.

'Phil, what are you…' Without finishing his sentence, Max Power dropped to his knees and peered beneath the truck to see the cover sitting into the hole. 'What the fuck?'

'Max, is everything okay with you?'

'That sewer was open, Phil. As God is my witness, that cover wasn't where it should've been. The lid was lying on the street.'

'Max, I would've seen an open manhole.'

Would he? Phil says he would've seen the open manhole, but Phil says lots of things. Phil once tried convincing Max that he had seen a ball bouncing up the stairs at a friend's house during a birthday party. Phil hadn't seen the third man — Fireman — bolt down the stairs. He should've crashed right into him for the love of Christ! It was quite possible that Phil missed that cover, too taken with the fire, and was lucky enough to drive over it…and even luckier to block it off from any potential accidents.

Max saw how his friend and workmate considered him. 'I'm not imagining it, Philly.'

'Like you didn't imagine a third person on fire in the house, running down the stairs by me? Don't you think I would've seen something like that, Max?' He paused. 'I know you, so don't take what I'm about to tell you the wrong way. I think you need a few days off. Burke,' referring to the boss, 'would only be too happy to oblige you. You've been on-call ever since I can remember. Are you ever not on-call? It's not all about the money, man. Go home and spend some time with Virginia and Danielle.'

Max didn't answer. He opened the toolbox section of the fire truck and from it took a manhole key. He was aware his friend was only trying to offer some solid advice, but he couldn't shake the feeling he was being condescended to. For the sake of their friendship and their stellar work record together, he held his tongue. But he drew the line at telling Phil that he was right, that it was all just his imagination. Max was as much convinced of the burning silhouette in the flames of that fucking horror house as spotting the open manhole, and if Phil thought—

His skin crept as he realised that someone had just been under the very truck he stood next to right now. In the moments between spotting the open sewer hole cover and calling over Phil, this prankster had levered the cover onto the access hole…without making a fucking sound. Whoever it was had heard him call Phil over. The notion that the strange person living under the street had heard his voice gave him the real heebie-jeebies. And he wasn't sure why. Max imagined a hand popping up out of the ground beneath the truck's exhaust pipe and pulling the cover over themselves. Extra chills in the knowing that whoever had done this was now below his feet in the sewer tunnels. And Max knew that dark, dank, wreaking place too well, having to go down there occasionally as part of his work routine.

Everyone climbed into the fire truck. As the wheels drove over the hole, Max stepped forward to have a closer look at the metal rim. It was just a manhole cover. No more, no less. He got down on one knee, almost as if he was about to propose to that cover. He jammed the hooked end of the lifting key into the pick hole and was about to pull up the lid when Phil called out, 'Max, it's been a long night and we want to go home. We still have to dry out the hose lines and load up the truck. Our face masks need to be inspected, cleaned and sanitised. The oxygen tanks need to be…'

'Fuck!' huffed Max and pulled the key from the manhole. 'I know the procedure, Phil!'

'You can come back tomorrow,' his friend suggested.

That wasn't a bad idea, thought Max. But he didn't know then that his night was only just beginning and tomorrow was very far away.

Dead End

Psst… Yes, you!

If you enjoyed this book, I'd appreciate it if you could take a minute of your valuable time to leave a rating/review at all the important places. Your feedback means a lot to me, and it will greatly help to encourage somebody to take a chance on a nobody like me ;)
Regards, Jon.

More horror novels:

2021
The Squatter

2022
Billy's Experiment

2022
Crazy Daisy

2023
Hotel Miramar

2023
Rosie

2023
Horror short story collection
Dead End Tales

2024
Drive

2024
Fireman

Printed in Great Britain
by Amazon